TALL TIMBER

Tall Timber

by

George Goodchild

Dales Large Print Books
Long Preston, North Yorkshire,
BD23 4ND, England.

British Library Cataloguing in Publication Data.

Goodchild, George
    Tall timber.

    A catalogue record of this book is
    available from the British Library

    ISBN   1-84262-212-9 pbk

Cover illustration © Len Thurston by arrangement with
P.W.A. International Ltd.

The moral right of the author has been asserted

Published in Large Print 2003 by arrangement with
Mrs S Roberts

Dales Large Print is an imprint of Library Magna Books Ltd.

Printed and bound in Great Britain by
T.J. (International) Ltd., Cornwall, PL28 8RW

CHAPTER ONE

Susan Lessing, head on hands, elbows propped on the dainty breakfast table, heeded as little the aroma of her coffee as she did the nodding, beckoning rows of hollyhocks outside the window through which she stared with unseeing eyes.

There was something besides coffee and hollyhocks on the mind of Susan Lessing, so much so that the girl who sat opposite, and whose own coffee was also untouched, had to speak twice before Susan, with a start, dropped her hands from her mop of bronze hair.

'Yes?' she queried of the dark, slightly older girl who sat behind the coffee urn. 'I beg your pardon, Edith – you were saying–'

'Quite a lot,' answered the other, a bit acidly. 'It all seemed so reasonable in the beginning, and–'

Susan sighed, as her gaze wandered again to the garden seeking what she had apparently not found before. She nodded. 'Yes, it did seem that if two can live as cheaply as one, as they are so fond of saying, that three could do just a bit better, especially if each could do *something.*'

More matter-of-fact Edith Chalmers smiled ruefully.

'I'll admit,' she said, 'that the theory was as right as such things usually are, but what's troubling me now, and I can see how it's troubling you also, is that if the postman doesn't show up with a letter soon I shall be a fit subject for a straitjacket, and what's more, if we don't get any answer at all to your letter to your Uncle Peter, that we might as well realize here and now that it is, as our one theatrical friend would put it, "curtains" for us.'

Again Susan Lessing, usually so light of heart, sighed as she turned to her neglected coffee. But thoughts were tumbling over each other as she nibbled at her toast with no thought for the bright morning sun that invited, or the slight breeze from the nearby sea that rustled the crisp curtains of the breakfast room in the small cottage that the girls for two years had called home.

She was right, she considered. So was Edith. The theory had been all right for two years, and given a better chance it might still be. Her wandering thoughts went back to the time they had come to the little cottage at Lifton-on-Sea, and the reasons for coming. There had, first, been the catastrophe. She shuddered, and her lip trembled as the memory came of the time when an Alpine disaster had robbed herself and Edith and

Peg Chalmers of their parents. Fate thus had thrown the three girls together, and from the first they had determined to remain so. Grim facts, too, there had been for them all to face, for it was not until they were trying to recover from the shock that it was made clear to them that each would have to make her own way in the world, as both the Lessing and Chalmers families had been impoverished in the war to an extent that the girls, still in school at that time, had not guessed. There had been, it is true, one alternative for Susan. Her uncle, Peter Lessing, had offered her a home, but she had declined the rather half-hearted offer, to throw her lot in with her friends.

'Besides,' she had confided, 'can you imagine anyone leading a life – a real life – anywhere in Uncle Peter's proximity?'

Edith and Peg had agreed with Susan, as they always did, though what they knew of Uncle Peter was only what Susan herself had told them.

And so they had started on their experiment. Matters at first had been settled with such expediency and so little trouble that it might have warned them, had they had any experience, of what they might later expect. They had even had no trouble getting just the right sort of little home, and though during the first year they were compelled to draw out almost all their small capital,

9

things had been looking up during the second year, for Edith had found a market for her sketches and Peg had actually sold a few short stories. They had almost come to the point of self-congratulation and the idea that they really could make their living, Edith and Susan by painting, and Peg by writing. Or at least, said Peg: 'If I can't get a chance to write my great novel just yet, still I'm sure we can make enough for bread and strawberries and clotted cream.'

Susan smiled indulgently as she recalled that the child, not yet up in the bright August sunshine, was nineteen. Her smile became tolerant as she considered her own great maturity of five years more.

Susan turned once more to let her gaze wander idly through the open window to their cherished garden as her thoughts tumbled over each other. She was remembering the solemn occasion on their first night in their new home when they had all sworn fealty to each other. She could hear Edith's cool voice as it had been then.

'Now, girls,' Edith had said gravely, 'we've at least made a start, and they said we couldn't. There's no reason we shouldn't make a go of it either, if each is willing to do her part. The most important thing, of course, is that we stick together. Is each one willing to swear not to forsake the others, until – er – I believe the proper thing in swearing is to say, "until death do us part," isn't it?'

And then, as solemnly as they had ever made oath to a secret society in the school days but so shortly past, Edith and Peg Chalmers and Susan Lessing bound themselves, one to the other. And the tea had been made, the curtains drawn, and the new life begun.

That had been two years before. And now – well, things had come to be very different in a short time.

Susan looked up at Edith suddenly as her eyes glanced at the vacant seat at the breakfast table.

'Peg not up yet?' she asked, in a tone that intimated she was saying something for the sake of something to say.

'She's not feeling quite as strong as she might yet,' apologized the sister of the absent one, but there was a trace of bitterness in the other girl's voice as she answered.

'Fine home-coming for the child, isn't it? Oh, if only you or I could do something–'

'You've done what you could, haven't you, dear?' queried Edith gently. 'None of us could foresee that Peg was going to be so seriously ill when she was, or that her operation would cost so much – and you've written to your Uncle Peter, haven't you?'

'Yes,' said Susan, and she passed her cup for more coffee, the first cup having somehow been dispensed with, 'I've taken what might be called a shot at the moon, but if you knew my Uncle Peter you'd know that I'm asking a favour of someone who could teach the man in the moon himself something about coldness and distance. Oh, well – was that the postman?' and she started up eagerly only to drop back into her seat as she recognized the rustling outside. 'Fooled again. It's only Peg,' she remarked. 'Now mind, not a word to her about how really hard put we are; she'd feel it so.'

The other nodded as she, too, recalled how it had been the illness of her sister that had brought the three to their present extremity, a real one with bills piled on bills and even their rent months in arrears. It was time to think of these, though, and Edith's usually cheerful countenance was drawn at the realization that their whole hope had come to the point of what they might expect from a crabbed elderly man she had never seen, and who didn't even know her or her sister.

Though she had been well and strong for quite a while now, Peg Chalmers was not of a mind so soon to abandon her prerogatives of convalescent, a matter she proved a moment later when she breezed into the breakfast room just as the other two had finished their last mouthful.

Susan tried to put on an air of cheerfulness.

'You're late,' she admonished, shaking her finger at the delinquent, who, in contrast to her sister and friend who were in freshly crisp morning dresses, wore her more comfortable invalid's negligee. 'Don't let it happen again.'

'Humph!' remarked Peg inelegantly, as she slid into her chair and without another glance at her companions ravenously attacked the bacon and eggs. It was not until the first pangs of her new appetite had been appeased that she noticed the silence of the two. She glanced sharply at them.

'Why the gloom?' she queried, and then in sudden remembrance, 'Oh, I forgot! You were expecting an important letter from that old uncle of yours, weren't you, Susan? Did it come?'

Two heads shook sorrowfully and Susan pursed her lips as her gaze wandered again to the garden.

'Well, it can't be as bad as all that, can it?' went on Peg. 'You were asking him for money, weren't you, Susan? What if it doesn't come, it won't be the first time we've looked for money that didn't come, will it?'

For a second Edith looked her blithesome young sister over. It seemed such a pity to tell her; she had been so sick, too. But still—

'Peg,' she began slowly, 'Susan didn't want me to tell you, but I believe it's best. You've asked us some questions. Well, there's just this about it, and it's better for you to know. If we don't hear from Susan's Uncle Peter – and we've been waiting for three days now – why – out we go, that's all!'

'No!' breathed Peg, and she lowered her coffee cup so that the liquid spilled over into the saucer as she stared from one to the other. 'And it's all my fault!' she went on, slowly realizing. 'If it hadn't been for that horrid operation–'

'Don't be silly!' advised Susan. 'How could it be any more your fault than anyone else's? You couldn't help being sick, could you, any more than we could help having our sketches returned?'

'But what are we going to do?' Peg almost wailed. 'Suppose it doesn't come at all?'

'Furnished rooms or something,' sighed Edith, and her gaze travelled around the cosy little room that she had come to look on as home.

The silence that followed was the natural one where there is really nothing to be said. They were roused by a gentle knock on the door. Three heads went up and three pairs of eyes stared into the passage down which the housekeeper moved slowly. A minute later the woman came in with a letter in her hand.

'This was left at Myrtle Cottage by mistake,' she explained.

'Idiot!' said Peg. Then eagerly to Susan:

'Open it, do!'

As the housekeeper vanished, Susan slowly slit the blue envelope, took from it its enclosure, and began to read – aloud:

MY DEAR NIECE:-

I once offered you a home and you refused it to lead an unnatural kind of existence which is, and always has been, distasteful to me. I still offer you a home and such comforts as my pecuniary circumstances will allow. That is all I have to say. I trust that your present misfortune will have led you to realize the folly of your ways.

Your affectionate uncle,
PETER.

Slowly Susan crushed the missive in her hand, hot tears of anger and humiliation filling her eyes as she tried to force them back. She attempted to speak cheerfully.

'That, I would remark, as our friend Dan Mainwaring might put it, seems to be distinctly that.' But her tone changed as she added bitterly: 'What a fool I was to write to him! I might have known what to expect.'

Peg was crying softly.

'And it's all my fault!' she sobbed. 'Oh, that wretched, wretched operation!'

'Don't be ridiculous, I tell you,' snapped Susan. 'It's no time for it. There's something else to think about. Anyway, we know the worst. What's to be done?'

'I – I have six sketches to offer,' put in Edith hopefully.

Peg sighed. 'They'll come back,' she prophesied.

'They came back the last time. Things are awful just now. Nobody has any money.'

'Rot!' ejaculated Susan. 'Some people have millions. You only have to go to London or even to Bournemouth to see it rolling down the street on four wheels.'

'Wish I could get a little of it!' sniffed Peg.

Edith had been sitting quietly thinking. She looked up suddenly, started to speak, but laughed instead.

'Well, what's the matter now?' queried Susan, who saw no reason for mirth.

'I had an idea, but it's so ridiculous I hardly dare mention it. Yet there's a lot to be said for it. By Jove, it's not bad, really!'

Edith's face became serious. She looked closely at her companions and exploded her bomb.

'Why couldn't one of us get married?'

Peg giggled, but Susan merely shrugged her shoulders.

'If one of us were so foolish, how would that help the others?' she asked.

'I mean a marriage of convenience – a rich marriage.'

'First find the rich husband.'

'But he need not be a millionaire. Some

man with income enough to allow his wife five hundred a year. Suppose you married a man who allowed you five hundred–'

'I!' gasped Susan in dismay.

'I'm only supposing. You could agree to pay the rent of this cottage, and you could come down here for long periods and live just as we live now. With no rent to pay, we could manage to drag along quite comfortably.'

'What about the man?'

'The man! It is no concern of his how his wife spends her pin money. Really, the idea isn't so bad, is it?'

'It's horrible,' said Susan, with decision. 'I should hate to take money from any man.'

'But you were willing to borrow some from your uncle,' said Edith.

'That's different.'

'How is it? A man's a man, whether he is husband or uncle.'

'But I don't want to get married.'

'Neither do I, but I'd be willing to risk it in the common interest.'

'I think it is a splendid idea,' put in Peg, who had been listening with shining eyes, 'and I'll be the victim myself. It was on my account that our savings were spent, and it's my duty to go through. I used to know a chap named Gregory who was awfully keen on me. I'll–'

Edith silenced her with a wave of her hand

and shook her head resolutely.

'Alan Gregory was married two years ago.'

'Married! Oh, the wretch! Never mind, I–'

'You'll do nothing,' retorted her sister. 'You are not in this at all. You're too young.'

'Don't be absurd – I'm nineteen.'

'Please don't quarrel,' said Susan. 'In any case, the idea is repulsive and impracticable. We've got to find some other way out of our troubles.'

'There is no other way,' sighed Edith. 'Even if we manage to keep the landlord at bay for a few weeks we shall never be able to settle all those outstanding bills. Why shouldn't one of us get married? Lots of people do and live happily ever after.'

Susan's lip curled. Even if the suggestion were practicable it certainly did not coincide with what she had come to believe were her unalterable standards. Conventions – all of them – she rebelled against, and in this category she placed marriage, although she admitted failure to find any alternative that would meet human needs.

'The proposal is odious,' she said loftily, 'because it turns us into men-hunters with no other object than a mercenary one.'

'Nonsense,' argued Edith. 'There are always opportunities for getting married, and though one may look at it from a purely business point of view, there is no reason why it shouldn't end happily. It isn't only the romantic marriages which are successful. If I were to marry a man in such circumstances, I should do my best to make him happy.'

'Then marry one,' said Susan shortly.

'It wouldn't be fair. None of us wants to be married, and if one of us has to, it ought to be by lot.'

'You mean you would be willing to gamble on it?'

'Yes.'

'So would I,' put in Peg eagerly.

'No,' insisted Edith firmly. 'It rests between Susan and me.'

Peg's clenched fist banged on the table. She was determined to be included in the swindle.

'I won't be left out,' she objected, as might have a child left out of a favourite game. 'If you try to leave me out I'll give the whole business away, and then we shall be as we were.'

'What do you say, Susan?'

Susan laughed without much hilarity. The scheme seemed mad enough, but yet, as Edith put it, there was a certain amount of promise in it.

'How can we decide who shall be the victim?' she asked slowly, still unconvinced.

'We can cut a pack of cards,' suggested Edith. 'Peg, where are those Patience cards?'

Peg ran lightly to a drawer and produced the cards. She shuffled them in her hands and flung them on the table. Susan bit her lip nervously as she stared at the backs of them. Edith, having cast all care to the winds, drew a card.

'Come on,' she urged. 'Show your pluck.'

Susan still hesitated, but Peg put out her hand and drew.

'Does the lowest lose?' she inquired, a little huskily.

Edith nodded, and Peg exposed a four with a forced little laugh.

'What have you drawn, Edith?'

'A jack.'

Susan made a slight sound with her lips and carefully selected a card. Without looking at it first, she turned it face upwards on the table. It was the three of hearts!

'You, Susan!' said Peg.

Susan nodded and sat down in the chair, staring before her as if she already saw the vision of the unknown husband. Edith came towards her and put her hands on her shoulders.

'You don't like the idea? Let me do it.'

But the head of the other girl shook slowly and finally.

'No,' she refused. 'Having gone so far I'll see it through. We'll save this dear little place if it kills me. The great problem is where to find a husband – quickly!'

CHAPTER TWO

There are those women and girls who, as Susan Lessing knew, looking upon marriage as the eventuality of all things, wait not on the order of their searching, but go about the matter in a business-like way. Theirs not merely to wait for the right man to appear. Theirs to go out and seek, and having sought and found, theirs to bring him into the net with as little trouble and as much expedition as possible. To Susan, believing herself such a staunch feminist that marriage was one of the things in life least to be desired, such a course was not in possibility.

By the mere flick of a card, though, the grinning goddess had chosen for her a course that, to say the least, was distasteful, so all she could do was to hope that the same goddess would hesitate a reasonable time in crossing her path with the man who was fated to be her husband. But Fate, having gone thus far, had no intention of leaving her job unfinished. Where others might have sought for a long time, Susan found her searching ready to hand, done for her in a coincidental fashion, as it were.

It was strange, in a manner, that Susan

Lessing should have met Douglas Tearle through Dan Mainwaring. For Dan had long ago concluded – without any encouragement on the part of Susan, it must be admitted – that when the time came that the girl should be married to anyone, it should be to himself. In a tentative way, Susan had considered this one suitor of hers after the pact the girls had made, and had at once dismissed him. Decidedly Dan wouldn't do – for many reasons – the chief one, of course, being that there wouldn't be any five hundred a year coming to her from him to give to her friends. They'd be lucky, she and Dan, if they had five hundred for themselves, and Dan would have to do better than he ever had before to raise this. At present he was trying to write, one of the many things he had done with varying failures, and the one novel he had submitted to Susan for her approval had done nothing to strengthen her belief that the man who so regularly proposed to her would ever set the world afire as an author.

Mainwaring had come to Lifton-on-Sea on one of his rather regular vacations, and, of course, had lost no time in hunting up Susan. It had been after his ninetieth, or thereabouts, proposal, and its inevitable refusal, that he had spoken of the races, little knowing that he was but the mouthpiece of Fate who had decreed that Susan Lessing should meet the man who was to become her husband at Goodwood races. Susan demurred. In spite of the pleasantness of a holiday, she did not feel that she or the girls should take the time.

But the grinning goddess whispered in her ear once more, and Susan Lessing agreed to the proposal.

'I met a fine chap at the hotel,' urged Dan. 'Canadian. Douglas Tearle. He has a good car which he can drive to suit even you. I'm asking him and we'll go in his car. You'll like him, too, in spite of the slathers of money he has.'

Though Susan's eyelids fluttered just a bit at the remark and her heart beat faster, Mainwaring did not notice.

'Immensely big chap, with a chest like a bull's and a voice like nothing on earth, but still the best of fellows,' had been Mainwaring's description of his new friend, Tearle, to the girls, and when they met the Canadian they realized that he tallied well with the description. Sitting at the steering wheel of his big car as he drove to Goodwood, he appeared to be of enormous stature. He was young, though, and he had a chin that spoke of pugnacity. Yet his actions were the antithesis of his looks. He seemed extraordinarily nervous when he met the girls, and blushed as one of them might, under other circumstances, when Susan had the temerity to look into his steel-blue eyes. Fate had it, too, that Susan should sit beside him on this first occasion of their meeting, and there was more than once glance passed between the sisters seated in the tonneau as they watched the two, the big shy man and Susan with her fair young beauty. For what Mainwaring told them of Tearle's wealth had escaped neither of them.

The narrow winding lane merged into the main road. Fields of corn slipped by and the wind beat on their faces as the note of the engine rose higher and the speedometer hand wandered around the dial. Throughout the swift and delightful journey Tearle did not speak a word beyond replying 'Yes' or 'No' to an occasional question from Susan. In many ways he seemed utterly different from any man she had ever met. There was something deep and unfathomable about him – something that savoured of the wild.

Within a few miles of the race-course they fell in with the vast procession of cars, carriages and pedestrians that was wending its way to the common destination. The pace reduced to a mere crawl as they commented on the gay pageant. Tearle, with his great hands on the steering-wheel, laughed deeply from time to time at some humorous remark from Peg or Mainwaring, but he seemed to have no conversation of his own, or, if he had, he preferred not to give voice to it.

That was Douglas Tearle as Susan Lessing and her friends knew him through all that first day's acquaintance.

Just as Susan had expected, but which she had hoped might in some way be avoided, the silent man was the chief topic of conversation that night when the girls were at last alone and free for their kimono chat over the events of the day. His name entered the conversation, too, in a way she would not have preferred. Edith was bemoaning the unlucky inspiration that had made them make a wager, only to see their choice left hopelessly at the post.

'What little idiots we were!' she moaned. 'And now here's a note from the grocer letting us know in no uncertain terms that we've passed the limit of credit, and we have scarcely a penny!'

'It was all Dan's fault,' said Peg fiercely. 'He said nothing about going into the enclosure. Still,' she added, less belligerently, 'I suppose it is no use blaming him 'specially, any more than that man Tearle. We might have realized he would do just that thing. Isn't he a queer man, though?' she mused.

'I didn't see anything queer about him!' defended Susan, surprised at herself at the feeling that took possession of her as she realized that she wanted to defend him. 'I don't suppose he's any different from other

25

men who have more money than they know what to do with!'

Edith glanced slyly at her friend, but she spoke to Peg.

'I'll tell you one thing about him,' she announced. 'He's mightily interested in Susan. It didn't take four eyes to see that.'

Susan turned on her almost angrily, her anger enhanced, perhaps, by her own realization that Edith spoke the truth. Silent as Tearle had been, she had not failed to notice his embarrassment whenever their eyes met. When he had said good-bye that evening, the big hand that held hers had trembled, and had retained its grip for a fraction longer than was necessary.

'You blush,' went on Edith mockingly. 'Proves it true and you know it.'

'If it were – I can't help it.'

'Help it! Why, it's the chance of a lifetime.'

Susan regarded her steadily, but her heart beat fast in her bosom as she divined what lay behind the words.

'What do you mean?' she asked slowly, as though not comprehending.

'Our pact – remember?' Edith's face grew serious. 'Isn't it rather fortunate our meeting Tearle? Something has to be done, and done quickly, if we are not to be turned out neck and crop.'

'You – you mean–?'

'Tearle is already half in love with you. The

slightest encouragement and–'

Susan's heart quailed at the significance. So Tearle was the man sent by Fate to solve their pressing difficulties. Well, why not? He was young, strong, apparently rich. She had no love to offer, but she could give him friendship. It was that or the break-up of their home. She turned to the two watchful girls, and spoke huskily.

'I want to think,' she said. 'I'll tell you in the morning.'

Lying awake in the neat little bedroom, watching the moon on the sea through the open window, she made her decision. Tearle was the man. She would do her part!

To Douglas Tearle, pawn of Fate and Fortune during the past few years, when an army career and the resulting loss of his whole fortune in the Canadian Northwest had reduced him even to the expediency of smaller speculation and racetrack gambling with a smaller capital in an effort to get back to that country, the whole thing that had now happened to him (and all within the three weeks' period in which he had known Susan Lessing) was remarkable. It had not taken him those three weeks to realize what had happened to him, either – he into whose life no woman had ever before stepped – for he had known it even on his first meeting, though more fully realizing the miracle before the end of the first week when the fire that had been smouldering in his bosom burst into flame. The exultation made all his former life seem insignificant.

There was but one flaw to his day-dreams as he sat one evening on the veranda of his hotel, looking out over the sea and catching through its haze glimmers of a wondrous future that might be. He was uncomfortable when he thought of Mainwaring. At first he had thought the boy merely a friend of all three of the girls at the cottage, but one event after another had brought to him the realization that Mainwaring loved Susan Lessing. It certainly complicated things, for Tearle had no way of gauging the girl's own feeling. To one thing he was not blind. Mainwaring had deliberately avoided him of late, and that was proof that the youth knew that he, Tearle, too, loved the girl.

He got up to pace the length of the veranda in his perplexity. He stopped as Mainwaring came through the door.

'Hold on, there!' he called, as the other made to go on as though not seeing him.

Mainwaring stopped short at the booming command.

'What's wrong?' he asked coolly.

Tearle approached and stood towering a good six inches above him as he spoke.

'I had an idea you were raw with me about something. If that's so, we'd better get it straightened out right now. Get it off your chest, sonny!'

Mainwaring flushed, but his surly answer accepted the challenge.

'We have conflicting interests,' he said icily. 'You know that!'

'I – think – I get you,' nodded Tearle. 'Well, what then?'

'It puts an end to any kind of friendship between us.'

'Humph!' snorted the big man. 'Queer idea of friendship you have, my boy! Competition's a healthy enough thing, I guess. What's to prevent you from going in and winning?'

'You.'

Tearle smiled quietly and shrugged his broad shoulders.

'Don't laugh!' snapped Mainwaring irritably. 'You have all the advantages and you know it.'

'Just what advantages, might I ask?' queried Tearle, still quietly, his eyes holding Mainwaring's.

'Money. You're rich and I'm penniless. If–'

A curious look entered Tearle's eyes.

'You appear to know a lot about my affairs,' he laughed grimly.

'I don't – as much as I should, perhaps,' answered Mainwaring meaningly. 'But I do know this. You are not of Susan's world. Oh, I don't mean that you are any the worse for

29

that, but you can't give her the things she wants–'

'Just now you said I could.'

'I mean spiritual things. Art, music, literature.'

'Perhaps they don't matter quite so much as you think,' was Tearle's thoughtful comment. 'The things that matter to my mind are square-dealing, sacrifice, courage when things look black. Perhaps I'm wrong. I'll admit I'm a rough kind of chap that can't tell art from canned beef, but from what I've seen of life the things that last are just the ordinary things like pluck and comradeship.'

A cynical smile was Mainwaring's only reply as he turned on his heel and left. Tearle watched him go.

'Rich!' he muttered. 'So that's it! Humph!'

Try as he might, he could not keep Mainwaring's remark from troubling him. In all his meetings with Susan, they had spoken little of his past or of what he might be now. She appeared to take him at his face value, and that was all he asked. As he thought of her – her charm, her beauty, the soft touch of her hand on his arm, the blood surged through his veins. The want of her, this one woman, the need of her, was a need far greater than any he had ever known; greater even than the call of the land where he had once wrested a fortune only to lose

30

it, but which had been calling him again.

Insistently Mainwaring's word swept through his mind. Rich! Suppose Susan thought so, too. Would it make any difference? He tried to banish the idea as disloyal, but it kept torturing with its insistence. Confound Mainwaring for rousing such unworthy thoughts!

CHAPTER THREE

Peg Chalmers was just finishing her tea in the living-room when Dan Mainwaring came in. That there was something troubling him was plain enough to see, and Peg believed she could give a shrewd guess as to the reason.

'Tea, Dan?' she offered, but the young man shook his head.

'No, thanks,' he declared. 'Just dropped in to say good-bye to you and Edith. I'm taking the night train.'

'But you must see Susan, too, surely,' insisted the girl. 'Have you seen her?'

Mainwaring nodded. 'Just left her finishing a masterpiece over in the meadow,' he said glumly, and would have gone on, but Peg started up.

'Oh,' she said, and the word held a world of understanding as she glanced at the disappointed face before her. 'I'll fetch her. I won't be gone a minute. Wait here. Edith'll be in in a moment! You don't mind?' And without waiting for an answer, she caught up her sun-hat and flitted from the room.

Restlessly Mainwaring waited. He felt that in all decency he must say farewell to Edith, but he had no mind to see Susan again. Peg had been only too correct in her surmise that he had just received his final congé, and the fact that Susan had begged that they remain on their former friendly basis had in no wise lessened the pain and disappointment of the refusal he knew this time meant for all time. And he felt he knew the reason why. Tearle.

Restlessly he wandered about the room. He was glancing at some sketches on a table when his glance fell on a small, leather-bound volume. Idly he opened it, but his first impulse was to close it again, for what he had taken to be an ordinary book was without doubt a diary of Peg's, packed with writing in her firm, small hand. But the great tempter of all must have been near the man's elbow then, for there could be no other reason for his eye falling on that one paragraph which made him cast aside all sense of decency and utter a low ejaculation of amazement. He had time for but a hurried scanning when he heard Edith's footsteps and the voice of a man – Tearle, he knew – and an impish grin of satisfaction crossed his face. As he turned at the opening of the door, the hand that held the book went to his coat pocket, and when he withdrew it, Peg Chalmers' cherished diary lay safely within.

He made no effort at friendliness towards the newcomer, and, in spite of Edith's urging, declined to stay for supper as Tearle accepted.

'No, I must be off to my packing,' he said stiltedly, as he started to go, then turned at the door. 'Oh, by the way, Tearle, I'll be wanting to see you before I leave. There is something important I must say – show you.'

Douglas Tearle did not like the look in the eyes of his former friend as Mainwaring hurried down the hallway. But he had completely forgotten the young man or anything he might have to say an hour or so later when he and Susan set off for an after-supper stroll by the sea.

They skirted the village and came out on the cliffs. The moon, which was at the full, had risen but half an hour before and was silvering the sea and the nodding wheat that grew almost to the cliff edge. Facing the moaning sea they sat on a fallen tree and for some time were strangely silent.

It was a night made for lovers, and Tearle felt the spell of it with such force as to make his brain reel. He had really come to tell her about himself, of his past and his hope for the future, but words were difficult to frame when his heart was leaping in his breast and her head was within a few inches of his shoulder.

'Susan!' he whispered suddenly.

'Yes.'

The response was so soft he scarcely heard it, but he knew her face was turned towards him and that the hand near him was trembling. He took it and held it tight. Hope soared when she made no attempt to withdraw it. Words bubbled to his lips and it needed all his self-control to sort them into intelligible order.

'Susan, I've got to tell you to-night – now that – that I love you as I've never loved anything before. If you don't want to hear it just say so and I'll go and not worry you again–'

'Don't – don't go,' she whispered.

'Then it's as good as said,' he replied joyously. 'I reckon I'm the luckiest fellow alive. Since that day when I first saw you I've done nothing else but hanker after you. At times I thought I was aiming too high. I'm a rough kind of fellow used to rough life. You're different; you've got the polish I've never had, but I'll get it if you want it.'

'It doesn't matter,' she murmured. 'You're you.'

'Sure I am. I can't tell you all the things I'm thinking. I reckon no man could do that. They're too big to put into words. But if you'll just trust me to do the right thing, to pull you out of any corner we may get into, to put you above every darned thing in this queer old world, I'll be happy.'

Her head nodded as if she, too, found words inadequate. It was so near to him that it was not strange that the next moment it lay on his shoulder. Then the fires within him broke loose. The big arms crushed her close to him and his lips rained kisses on hers.

An hour that seemed but a fleeting moment had gone before, dazed and speechless, he stood outside the garden gate with his two hands grasping hers.

'Good night,' she murmured. 'Don't come in. I – I want to tell them – alone.'

He thought he understood and kissed her once again before he went bounding homewards on wings of unimagined happiness. She loved him – she loved him! That thought was big enough to overleap all other considerations. If she loved him what matter an uncertain future? Together they would beat the whole world. Nevertheless he was determined to place her in possession of all the facts that she might know exactly the kind of fight they had to put up. And, of course, she must be willing to wait. She would, too, because she loved him; had told him so. His feet had wings as he strode over the ground that took him away from Susan and to – Mainwaring!

Inside the cottage, Edith and Peg waited with suppressed excitement the return of Susan. Young as they were, something in Tearle's eyes and the way he had looked at Susan when the two had gone off after supper had told their woman's instinct what to expect. The way their chatter was bitten off short at Susan's entry proved that they had been talking about her, but she had rather expected that, too. She came towards them, slowly removing the light wrap that covered her shoulders, knowing that she must tell them, but rather doubting her ability to make them understand. For all that had happened within the last hour had come with a surprising shock to her. Something had happened to her on that walk with Tearle; something she had deemed impossible. What she really wanted to do was to go straight to her room and reflect on the miracle, but she knew that first she must have something to say to them.

It was Edith who spoke first.

'Something's happened,' she announced oracularly, nodding. 'Tell us, Susan! Has he proposed?'

'Has he?' echoed Peg, eagerly.

Susan nodded. 'Practically,' she admitted.

Edith sank back into her chair with a sigh.

'Thank heaven!' she murmured. 'I was afraid you were going to fail us at the critical moment.'

The flush of happiness that had dyed Susan's face faded to waxen whiteness.

'You're thinking of that wretched pact?' she asked, coldly.

'Of course,' replied Edith, wondering. 'Why, what's the matter, Susan?'

'You've got to forget it,' said Susan with firmness. 'I've finished with it. I don't care what you may think of me! I won't have anything to do with it!'

'But you said he–'

'Yes, he does love me. And he believes in me, trusts me, too. When I began this I didn't see where it was going to end. I didn't imagine I should – I should–'

Peg gleaned the remainder of the unfinished sentence and her jaw fell with astonishment.

'You don't mean you have fallen in love with him?'

'I – I believe I have.'

'All the better,' Edith remarked as she laughed amusedly. 'It makes things easier. It need not alter our agreement in the least. All that has happened is that you have found a real fiancé instead of a convenient one.'

'It makes just this difference,' retorted Susan, 'that I absolutely refuse to have anything to do with that disgraceful agreement. From this moment I consider myself freed from it.'

'And free from your obligation to us?' asked Edith, eyebrows lifted.

'Edith!' remonstrated Peg. 'If Susan feels that way it would be horrid for us to want to go on with it.'

'I don't see that the position is changed in the least. If Susan says plainly that she intends to cut us–'

'No, no,' interrupted Susan. 'Why do you say such unkind things? You know it will be a pleasure for me to help you in any way I can.'

Edith nodded and took Susan's hand to express her regret at the harsh words.

'What are we really quarrelling about?' she asked.

'Motives,' replied Susan softly. 'If I marry Tearle it will be because I – I love him – that and nothing else. Unless you accept that I will break it off to-morrow.'

Edith, who was, above all, logical, saw not the slightest objection.

'Very well,' she said. 'But how did it all come about?'

'I don't know,' replied Susan with a shake of her head. 'It was not until this evening that I realized how hateful the whole thing was – the mercenary side. He is so different from anyone I have ever met before. There is something so amazingly simple about him. When I thought of what I had set out to do it made me so ashamed I – I couldn't look into his eyes.'

She stared through the curtains out at the moon under which but a short time before she had sat and listened to the man's deep voice saying things as no other man had ever said them. Nor could another have aroused within her bosom that quick throb like a burning flame.

'It's wonderful to think of your being in love, Susan,' sighed Peg with a short laugh.

'I suppose it is, especially after so much cheap cynicism has been vented on the subject. I didn't know what life meant until this came. It is the greatest thing that ever happened to me. Now laugh if you want to, Edith!'

But Edith did not laugh, for she could see the seriousness in the big wistful eyes of the woman who loved Douglas Tearle, eyes that were even then looking far off into the future and hoping that it was for something more than the beauty of her face and form, which she could not but acknowledge, that the man to whom she had given her heart cared for her; and hoping, hoping, that she could live up to the greatest of the ideals.

Daniel Mainwaring and Douglas Tearle faced each other in the latter's hotel room across a space of three feet. The former spoke, half sneeringly.

'You are a man who believes in truth, I take it,' he asked, 'no matter how much it hurts?'

'Go on,' snapped Tearle tersely. 'I don't get you yet.'

'You will in a minute,' sneered Mainwaring. 'I'm going to show you something that will hurt like the devil. Can you stand it?'

'I reckon I'm big enough to stand most things,' grunted Tearle. 'Get on with it.'

Mainwaring shoved his hand into his coat

pocket and brought forth a small un-lettered, leather-bound book. He shoved it at the big man.

'Then take this and be hurt, damn you!' he cried exultantly, and before Tearle could either reply or ask what it was all about, the other, with a nasty laugh, was out of the door.

For some minutes Tearle stood staring at the book without opening it. Something seemed to tell him that what he would find were it opened would change his life. But the grinning devil of the book had not deserted it. Even though he had never seen a diary, he knew at once that he was gazing at one, and his first instinct, too, was to close it. But the devil had no such intention. He turned Douglas Tearle's eyes to a paragraph which no man on earth, situated as he was, could have withstood.

At the end of an hour, he who had been the simple-minded man of the open country was still reading. Slowly he closed the fateful book, he who was a man changed. He stared straight ahead at nothing, but seeing many things.

'Framed,' he mused, and his lips that knew best how to smile their slow smile were set in a grim straight line. For a long time he sat there without moving. The bolt that had descended had broken through his complaisance, laying bare the injured heart of him. His childhood, all his former life had been spent in a land and an environment to nurture pride and self-respect. The man had been up against the big things of life a hundred times, even before he had been through the war. A few times they had beaten him, temporarily, but they had never laid upon him such ignominy as now tortured him. His battles before had principally been with Nature. And Nature, however cruel, however relentless, played fair, without trickery or subterfuge.

Now a woman had hurled the gauntlet, challenging to battle by wits. His first impulse had been to refuse that form of fighting; to go to her and shame her into repentance. But that seemed futile and inadequate. The more he thought of it, the more he was impelled towards fighting with the weapons that the little book made most plain that she had chosen. But there was to be no pleasure in it, no peace of mind; for above all flamed the knowledge that he had loved her – loved her still. And he had thought she loved him, God help him!

He roused himself at last as the new thought came and the lips were set in a line that none who knew him would have recognized.

'Well, she's called the tune,' he muttered. 'I guess she'll have to pay the piper.'

CHAPTER FOUR

For a man whose chief communion all his life had been with the outdoors, and so a devotee of truth and plain dealing, Douglas Tearle found himself playing a most unaccustomed rôle during the days preceding the marriage which was hurried at his own insistence. Having made up his mind to go through with the affair, no matter what the evidence of the damning diary, he had determined that the climax should come swiftly.

He was surprised at his own ability to play the affectionate lover as he seemed expected to play it. But no more surprised than he was at what he believed Susan's consummate acting. That she did not love him, never had loved him, but was after the money she imagined him to have, he was assured. It was hard to believe, though, when he looked into her clear, steady eyes. His own part he found difficult enough, so much so that at times it was all he could do to go on with it and not take refuge in flight, but the way Susan was carrying her part out filled him with amazement. Lies, lies, all lies, he thought grimly, then he set his teeth in that same old tight line and he thought of the time when it would be his innings.

Once he asked her: 'Only two days more, Susan. Are you still willing to take the risk?'

She breathed deeply, the light shining through those clear eyes. In his blindness, the man could not know how much she meant her reply when it came – how all her former life had become as nothing; now in the glory of her new experience she had time to think of nothing but a roseate future with the man she loved.

'Wonderful, isn't it?' she breathed. 'And of course I want to take the risk as you call it. For better or for worse, as they say, don't they, though I'm sure there can be no worse with us.'

'But you know so little of me.'

'That is part of the blessed mystery. I want to discover all about you afterwards. I know as much as a prospective wife ought to know if she has any romance in her being. I know this; that you're big and dependable, and – and – lovable.'

'And that's all that matters?' There was a hint of a cynical smile in the eyes bent piercingly on her, but he could see no trace but the truth (more power to her acting, he thought) in the girl's own eyes as she answered: 'I think so.'

That Susan had never asked him about his business or his income convinced Tearle that on these points she was already satisfied. The big car and the expensive hotel had done their share well, he thought, with an inward bitterness as he remembered how that car, an expensive speculation that had proved a white elephant, had already been sold for a distant purpose he had in mind.

Only once did Susan speak of the future.

'Douglas,' she asked him as they returned from a stroll along the cliffs one day, 'have you thought about where we are to live – after?'

'Can't you leave that to me?' was his reply, for already he believed he knew what her remark was leading up to.

'Well, I – I think I ought to have at least a say in the matter,' urged the girl.

'Where would you like to live?' he queried.

'Somewhere near here, I think. I want to keep up my painting, and I want to be near the girls. We've been such comrades and we all started out together.'

'If we would be happiest here,' Douglas answered, after a pause, then he laughed as he believed he had given the necessary diplomatic answer that bound him to nothing.

If he believed so, however, Susan had garnered a different impression. When she left him she hurried to Edith and Peg, both busy with the last of the simple trousseau for the forthcoming event.

'Oh, girls!' she explained. 'He's promised! We're to live near here, and I'll have you, and besides, most of all, I'll have him!'

'Was it hard to get him to agree?' asked Edith, snipping off a thread and holding out a filmy garment for a critical inspection.

Susan spoke proudly.

'He would naturally want to do what I wished, if he loves me, and I know that he does. Besides, he's promised!' From her tone, Susan seemed to be adding that this would settle all things.

Had she seen the man of her thoughts and prideful boasts though, as she made them, her ideas might have had less of a roseate and far more of a sombre cast. For Douglas Tearle at that moment, having but a few moments before left the girl he was to marry, was standing on a cliff gazing out towards the sea, towards the Canada of his childhood and dreams. He pulled a small leather-bound book from his pocket and mechanically his fingers found the well-known, well-thumbed page. His eyes turned from the horizon to see the dancing blurred words in Peg's small handwriting. Yes, there it was. There could be no mistake. In spite of Susan's insouciance, here was the proof that all she said, all she did was acting. He read:

July 11. – Uncle Peter has replied at last. Nothing doing! What a blow to this pestered, impecunious household! Edith has a brain wave (most natural for Edith). One of us must get married to a man of means and undertake to support the other two until such a time as Fame or Sudden Death arrives. Susan in a state of nervous prostration, and I with the sensation of a cold sponge down my spine.

We actually summoned the courage to face the situation, and poor Susan was the victim. Will she have the pluck to carry it to the bitter end? I wonder–

The man's eyes blurred, but he flicked the pages to another well-remembered spot that stood out before the tortured eyes of his mind in letters of fire. Peg had written:

July 25 – Glorious Goodwood! What an experience! We lost our heads, our reputation, and our money, and all through Dan Mainwaring. But in another direction Fate has been kind. I verily believe we have found 'the man,' or at least Susan has. Big, solemn, plenty of the necessary. I fancy I can lay my hands on the future Mrs Tearle–

Slowly, painfully, Tearle lifted his eyes from the written page to gaze once more longingly out at sea. The pity of it! And to think that even now, tricked, cheated as he knew himself to be, he wanted the girl still – must have her. To abandon his project would be no solution to his mental problem. He must go on – on!

Unconsciously his great hands crushed the little leather-bound book that had spelled disaster to him. He muttered a deep oath as his arm rose and he flung the hateful thing far out to sea.

For a man but so recently married, one whose happiness is supposed to have begun, Douglas Tearle was acting most peculiarly.

Susan, but a few hours Mrs Tearle, was becoming a bit bewildered. She had first noticed his strange actions during the channel crossing to France but a scant hour after their marriage. They had continued during the tedious journey to Paris, whence they were bound for a honeymoon trip. The newly made wife had been able to get but little out of her husband. He had replied civilly enough to her queries, but in his face and manner there was distinctly something that dampened the joy and excitement she had so confidently expected.

Just before dinner time they arrived in their hotel in Paris. To Susan's intense astonishment, Douglas steered her to a distinctly third-class hotel in a back street, far from the boulevards. When she was shown to her room she saw that it was a single room, and she suffered a further shock on learning that her husband's room was on another floor and far away from her.

It was all strangely discomfiting.

Evening dress, in such a place, was, of course, out of the question, so Susan decided on one of her oldest frocks, in which she presently presented herself to her husband, whom she found sitting in the lounge wearing a grey suit and a soft collar. So preoccupied was he with his thoughts in which he was sunk, that he did not see her until she touched him on the shoulder.

'Ready?' he asked, getting up slowly.

The dinner, like most French dinners, was good, but the tone of the place jarred on the bride. It was gloomy and the table linen was not too clean. Tearle, however, appeared not to notice anything amiss, but went on with his dinner. Susan, though, soon found herself too perturbed to eat. She stopped idling with her cheese after what seemed an interminable time for a meal, and leaned across towards her husband.

'I – I don't think I feel well, Douglas,' she said, plaintively. 'Won't you please take me upstairs? Besides,' she added, with an appealing glance at the man, which he did not see, 'I want to talk to you, Douglas.'

Silently he bowed as he rose and guided her to the dingy steps and to her small room where Susan's things lay flung about in feminine disorder as she had left them after her hurried dressing. She dropped into a chair by the window, but Tearle continued to stand, waiting apparently somewhat impatiently for what it was she might have to say. There was that in the man's attitude that showed he believed the time had come to face the issue, and his jaw stood out as the grimness (the new grimness of his lips) accentuated his newborn stubbornness.

For a moment Susan continued to stare out of the window at the none too attractive side-street scene. Then she lifted her eyes to Tearle.

'Douglas,' she said, timidly, shyly, 'I – I wanted to ask you, is there – is anything the matter? You are so – so silent, and acting so queerly. And then this place! It's deadly! Why did you bring me here?'

His answer was grim, cold. 'I'm sorry if it's not what you're used to. But it's the best we can afford.'

'But surely' – surprise was in her voice – 'you are not so–'

'So poor as not to be able to give you something better?' he finished for her. 'I am. It took most of my money to buy the boat tickets.'

The surprise was so great as well as sudden that Susan could only gaze at him for a moment with astonishment, her jaw dropped. It was not that she cared for the money part at all; rather the suddenness and the raw way it came from this man she had thought rich, but so thinking, hadn't cared at all one way or the other.

'The boat tickets!' she murmured, wondering. 'A mere channel crossing—'

'No!' snapped Tearle, determined to have it over and done with at once. 'I don't mean the channel crossing. I mean our boat tickets for Canada. We're going there in the morning – to live.'

'Douglas!' Susan could not take it in. Surely he must be making some sort of a grim jest. Canada! Of all places! But he couldn't mean it. Besides—

'But, Douglas, dear,' she began, inclined to be wheedling if he should be joking, 'you promised, you know – Lifton, and the girls—'

'Promised, did I?' he repeated, and the colour mounted to his big face as he remembered that odious volume once more. 'Well, just think it over, my dear, and remember, whether I promised or not. Yes, you asked me, but if you'll recall, I said distinctly that we would live there if we would be happiest there. We! And "we" most certainly does not mean you entirely. I'm part of that "we". And I'll be happiest in Canada. That's where I belong. And I'm going there because I'm down and out and have no prospects anywhere but in the country in which I was born. Out there there's work for a man like me, and that's where we're going – you, my wife – and me. Now you have it, so make the best of it!'

He started to turn and leave her, but her low voice stopped him.

'Are you sure I am?' she asked, and her quick brain was thinking. Susan Tearle was trying to save her fast-tumbling house of dreams. This revelation of Tearle's real self had come with such unexpectedness. He whom she had thought so noble, so fine, to trick her! To wait until now to reveal himself. Slowly she felt the warm tingle that had been hers since she first knew she cared for him turning to an icy chill. He had been fooling her! Did not mean what he said! Perhaps he had not meant any of it! To a girl of Susan Tearle's calibre a promise was a sacred thing, and its breaking meant more than other things could atone for. The curt way in which he had informed her of his circumstances, the fact that he had no money when she had thought he had meant nothing. It was that broken promise that hurt, and the fact that it was, in her mind, the precursor of dire prophecies of worse to come. Her brain was working at express speed, and even while he spoke and she considered, she could feel the cold dread hand that was crushing from her heart all love for the man who could so make sport of her, chilling, killing it all, she believed.

Her voice was as cold as the hand on her heart as she went on:

'And you expect me to go to Canada with

you? With a man who has deliberately broken his promise to me so soon? You, who have acted a lie–'

'I never told you I was rich,' put in Tearle sullenly, but Susan waved him to an imperious stop.

'I don't mean that, as you very well know, in spite of your own littleness of mind,' she said coldly. 'It is the fact that you saw fit deliberately to trick me and to make a promise you never had any intention of keeping. May I ask on what grounds you expect me to accompany you to Canada?' she ended, with uplifted brows, and all the hauteur she could command.

'We're married!' said Tearle, with finality, as though that made an end of further argument, but he shuffled uneasily before the blazing-eyed, indignant woman who faced him. Slowly she looked him up and down a moment.

'You are not the man I married,' she declared. 'He was fine and just – not a breaker of promises.' Then her voice wavered a little and she turned to pick up and finger a glass that lay on her toilet table that he might not see her eyes as she gave him her decision. 'You must know, of course, Douglas,' as calmly as the turbulence of her feelings would admit, 'that this means the end of things. It has altered everything–'

'What has altered everything?' he broke in

irritably. 'The fact that I'm poor? That I can't dress you in silk and buy you motor-cars?'

In spite of herself, Susan winced under the words that hurt as no previous words had done, but she pressed back the hot tears of anger that rushed to her eyes as she tried to speak calmly.

'If you knew me – really knew me – you would know how impossible it is for me to forgive deception, and I can never forgive yours. I took you for an honourable man, a man who would scorn a lie–'

'I've never lied to you,' he growled. 'You took me on my face value and I guess you'll have to take the consequences.'

'Consequences! I refuse to recognize any consequences. Our ways lie apart.'

'Another mistake, my dear Susan,' he told her firmly. 'Our ways lie close together. Whatever there is to face we're going to face it side by side. We're partners in a concern that doesn't allow quitting.'

'You must be insane to talk like that. This is the end! I – I made a mistake and I'm going to take the only remedy. To think I should have been so blind!'

'I was blind, too, for a bit,' he muttered, meaningly, but Susan did not understand, for good reason.

His voice softened a little. 'Susan, there's no remedy you can take now; it's too late–'

'It's never too late to retrace a wrong step!'

she declared with spirit. 'To-morrow I am going back to England.'

'To-morrow by this time you and I will be heading for Canada. Facts are mighty hard things, and it's best to face them.'

'I'm used to facing facts,' she retorted with flashing eyes. 'Perhaps I've faced more than you imagine, but there are some things impossible to sit down under, and this is one of them. To live with a man one does – does not love–'

'So you admit that?'

'Y-yes.'

'It makes no difference.'

His composure, when her own heart was so hurt, aroused her deepest resentment.

'No difference!' she cried. 'It makes all the difference between Heaven and Hell. Anything would be preferable to a life of serfdom, bound to a husband who is lost to all sense of chivalry, even decency. You think you are going to drag me behind your chariot to any place you choose to select. Very well, I tell you now I will not come.'

She turned quickly from him to the window to hide the emotion she did not wish him to see, but which even her pride could not master. Douglas Tearle stopped at the door, his hand on the turning knob.

'I think you will,' was what he said, but his words held a deep meaning. 'No matter how you hate me, you're my wife. You can't alter that. And where I go, there you go too!'

The door closed upon him with a finality that accorded well with Susan's feeling that she had reached the finality of all things. In her heart she was assured that instead of loving the man who was her husband, she hated him. Confused on the borderland of that plane which so connects the emotions of love and hate, she felt that all her tenderness had turned to loathing. The future – she dared not think of it. Some way, though, she knew she must gather up the broken threads the best way she could. And then–

The flood of tears that Susan Tearle shed on the third-class pillow on the third-class bed of her third-class hotel bedroom had fully expended itself before she could think calmly enough to plan. She sat up, hair disordered, face flushed with weeping, all that a bride should not be, to think more calmly. There was this about it. Her husband did not love her. She felt sure she hated him. She could not imagine why, but he had sought to crush her with humiliation by forcing her to take a step against her will after calmly breaking a promise to her.

Tears once more – those of self-pity this time – rose to her eyes as she pictured how different things might have been had Douglas not deceived her. Her love for him had been great enough to have faced any privations by his side. This dingy hotel, for instance; the voyage to Canada with all its doubtful prospects. How different things would have been had not her love and faith been so cruelly shattered!

Perhaps it was as well for Tearle, walking the streets through that long night after he had taken his first step in his planned course of retribution, that he knew nothing of the streak of stubbornness that was stored away in his wife, along with her sweetness and charm and apparent malleability. Perhaps as well that he did not know how her own night's vigil and brooding had imbued her with a strength to fight him relentlessly with all the weapons she possessed. For Susan reasoned that if there had even been any love left, it was now entombed in this new influx of resentment and fighting spirit.

By the time the first faint streaks of dawn crept through the slits in the heavy curtains, she had made her plans. She reached under her soaked pillow for her bag and counted her money. There was sufficient to take her to London.

Though she was well aware that the Calais train did not leave till noon, she was packed, dressed and out of her hotel before her continental breakfast had been served. She was determined to take no chance of seeing Douglas.

She breathed a sigh of relief as the taxi rolled away towards the Gare du Nord.

Nevertheless her heart felt strangely moved at this silent departure from the man who had so short a time before meant more to her than anything else in life. That he should have proven false, a charlatan, was something she could not understand. Yet there it was and tears were idle.

Having a considerable time to wait at the station, she took breakfast at the buffet, after which she rounded up her luggage and had it put into a first-class compartment of the Calais train, which had just steamed into the station. There was yet a good hour before the train was due to leave, so she went for a stroll through the streets.

Her first shock of the morning occurred on her return. Standing outside the station was a taxi, and on the front of it were two large trunks which were strangely like her own and bore her initials. She stopped and examined them more closely. By several marks and scratches on the boxes she identified them.

'Where did you get that baggage?' she asked the sleepy driver indignantly.

'My fare just brought them from the station.'

'Your fare? Where is–?'

There was no time to finish the question, for the tall figure of Tearle approached her from behind and swung the door of the taxi open.

'You brought it to the wrong station,' he

growled. 'My luggage has gone on. Get inside!'

'How – how dare you!'

'Get inside.'

She felt her arm gripped as in a vice and found herself being propelled through the open door. Then it slammed, and the vehicle moved forward with a jolt. Tearle sat opposite her with his arm leaning on the window and his face impassive.

'You – you brute!' she ejaculated.

'Why didn't you wait for me?'

'I told you I was not coming.'

'Yet you are here.'

'Yes, but when the taxi stops I shall call a – a gendarme–'

He wrinkled his brows and gazed at her in his searching manner.

'Susan, I guess you're feeling raw, and I'll admit it's low-down for a man to drag a woman where she doesn't want to go. But I reckon I have different ideas from you about a good many things, and one of them is that where a man is, there ought his wife to be also.' He stopped a moment, but Susan, too infuriated to speak, did not reply. 'Better accept that theory,' he advised calmly. 'It'll save a lot of trouble.'

'I'll never accept anything from you,' choked Susan passionately. 'And – I'll – never – forgive – you!'

Susan Tearle was to discover that to escape

was easy in theory, but difficult in practice. Vigilant as she was, Tearle was still more so, and not once did she get the slight chance for which she hoped. Of course, she reasoned, as they at last approached the liner, she could make an outcry, a disturbance, when he made her go aboard. But her common sense vetoed that. She firmly believed that Tearle would pick her up bodily and carry her on the ship if she rebelled, and her pride revolted at the idea of a scene. She must look for some other way – later.

The big liner bound for Halifax went from Cherbourg that night, and aboard her were Mr and Mrs Douglas Tearle. In the darkness, as the monster made her way through the shipping, and out into the choppy channel, Susan Tearle sat in the bows, staring westward through the darkness. Hours passed, but still she remained motionless. It was close upon midnight when she heard a step behind her and turned her head to see Tearle looming up like a great phantom.

'Susan,' he whispered softly, and the tenseness of his voice proved he, too, had thought long, and was wearied. 'Susan,' he repeated, 'if we can be nothing else, can't – can't we be friends?'

The woman rose and shivered as though struck by a blast of cold wind. She spoke no word, but walked past him, and down to her cabin.

CHAPTER FIVE

On the fringe of a virgin forest under the gaunt Rocky Mountains, a man and a woman sat by the side of a campfire, clearing up the remnants of a meal. Fifty yards away, a river ran through a ravine. Moored to its near bank was a canoe. The campers were Tearle and Susan, and the canoe and its contents, plus the gear distributed about the fire, represented their stock-in-trade. Tearle took a linen bag from beside him and weighed it in his hand reflectively.

'Flour's getting short,' he remarked.

Susan glanced at the sack, nodded her head, and with her hands full of enamelled plates and cups, went down the steep bank to wash them. Tearle put down the flour-bag and gazed after her with wrinkled brows.

'Feeling raw again,' he muttered.

Two months had passed since they had entered Canada, and in those two months nothing had happened to alter their relationship. Such conversation as passed between them was of a purely business nature, having reference to the supply of food or ammunition. Gradually Susan had come to consider herself a partner, but an unwilling partner, in a not too prosperous concern. In appearance she was greatly changed, for the long skirt had given place to a shorter and more durable article, and thick boots replaced high-heeled shoes. Her coat was of buffalo skin, boasting large side pockets in which was a strange assortment of things from a clasp knife to a ball of string. Sun and winds had browned her face, but out of the wild nomad life she had gained wonderful physical fitness even in two months.

Tearle on his return to Canada had attempted to take up farming, but without capital the only opening for him was that of labourer, in which he saw no future worth considering. Skilled with the rifle and in the art of trapping, he had embarked on a business which at least offered freedom if not large profits.

They left the railroad at Calgary, purchased such gear as was necessary to the business at hand, and made across country by river routes. To Susan, the whole thing had been like a nightmare. She had followed him because she saw that the alternative was in being dragged along, and the former method was less injurious to her pride than the latter.

In several ways, however, his conduct had puzzled her. Apart from the dogged determination to enforce his will upon her, he was in every way accommodating. When the daily trip had been long and fatiguing, he had refused to let her help him in making ready the camp for the night, and had denied himself many things that she might be comfortable. She came to realize that his strength and experience were at her service, and to feel a sense of blessed security even amid the most alarming conditions.

But the feeling of servitude was always with her. In the deep woods, on the mountain tops, on the rushing rivers the consciousness of being a bond-slave was overwhelming. It stopped her from opening her arms to the sun, from feeling such gratitude to the call of the wild as her husband evidently experienced. But all the time she was subconsciously thankful he was what he was – a man of great strength of character whose life was at the service of a weaker creature.

She came back from the river to find him cleaning one of the rifles. On the ground beside him, a rough bundle was roped ready for transport. She slipped the plates inside a bag and looked at him inquiringly.

'I'm going to run down the river and try the woods on the northern bank,' he informed her.

'Beaver?'

'No, bear. There ought to be a grizzly or two round about. Will you take the small bundle?'

She nodded and picked it up, while he slung the rifle over his shoulder and attended to the rest of the gear. The shallow canoe was pulled inshore and the baggage placed aboard with the skins and tent which the craft already contained. Susan crept forward and took one of the paddles while he cast off the mooring line and with the agility of a cat took a seat in the bows.

A dip of the paddles sent the craft towards the centre of the swift stream. It gathered pace and the paddles were merely needed to guide it through the dangerous avenues of rocks over which the water broke in creamy foam. On either side the incomparably beautiful river banks slid by. Silver beech overhung the rugged rocks and behind them towering conifers mounted the steep embankment and went all the way up the mountainside until they ceased in an almost perfect horizontal line above which no timber grew.

'Look at that,' shouted Tearle. 'There's nothing like that outside Canada.'

She turned her eyes to the north bank, where a valley had opened between the bluffs revealing a vista of such marvellous beauty that she could not check an utterance of deep admiration. Above the normal drone of the running water came a deeper boom, which increased as they annihilated space.

'What is that?' she shouted.

'Rapids!'

They had never been down the river before, and the extent of the fall was unknown. She saw Tearle's muscles bulge as he tried to drive the canoe towards the nearer bank, and put her own paddle down to assist him. But he misjudged the speed, and the craft was carried past the opening in the rocks. A smash was avoided by a few inches and the canoe was headed for the centre of the stream again.

'We'll have to take it,' cried Tearle. 'Can't get inshore. Keep your paddle out and leave it to me!'

She did as he told her, but her heart felt cold as the noise of the falls grew louder and louder. The canoe swung round a bend and before her she saw a cloud of spray dancing in the sunlight. The pace increased, the wind sung in her ears. Rocks loomed up and were negotiated with miraculous skill.

'Don't move!'

She never heard the words, for the water suddenly dropped away at an appalling angle and out of it towered two gigantic spurs of rock with scarcely more than a yard between them. Down this channel the water literally roared, leaping over the walls on either side in its fury.

She saw death plainly written on the face of that awful water chute, and her hands gripped the sides of the craft as its nose went down. There was no time to think. The slim canoe shot through the channel like a rifle bullet. It hit the leaping mass of water beyond, quivered and rose in the air. Through the mist she suddenly saw a tongue of rock rushing at her.

'Sit still!' yelled Tearle.

But the warning came too late. She moved her body violently to avoid being hit and upset the balance of the canoe. The next instant she was out of it and water was thundering in her ears. She thought that the death she had seen written so clearly had come. In the minute or so of consciousness that remained all her former life was relived, every little incident clear-cut. She fought with her arms and legs, but her swimming powers were restricted to a few strokes and her strength was futile against the fury of the stream. She grew icy cold, and a strange sleepiness came over her.

Tearle righted the canoe almost by a miracle, and searched the welter of water for some signs of his wife. He put all his strength into the paddle and drove down-stream at a tremendous pace. A moment later he managed to send the craft through an opening towards the bank and beached it, then leaped madly across the rocks towards the main current.

His one hope was that Susan had missed collision with the death-dealing rocks under the surface and he watched in dreadful suspense for some sign of her. A minute passed, then another – then a hundred yards below him he saw a saturated head appear for a second. Catching his breath he dived and made towards the spot with powerful over-arm strokes. He reached it and plunged into the water with his eyes open, but though the sunlight penetrated to the rocky bottom he saw nothing but stones and the débris of ages.

Down the stream he went again, diving every few seconds, only to meet with bitter disappointment. The last shred of hope was departing when round a bend on the bank he saw two mules and the smoke of a camp-fire. As the stream carried him onwards, the figure of a man came to view, then another; last of all a prone shape near the two men.

'Hello there!'

The taller of the two men had seen him and was waving to him. He struck out for the bank, and scrambled ashore. The man who had waved stared at him and then pointed to the prone figure in the clearing.

'We've got her. Were you looking for her?'

'Yep. Is she–?'

'She's coming to. Had a narrow squeak, I reckon.'

Tearle made across the intervening space and halted by the side of the unconscious Susan. He was sinking to his knees beside her when she opened her eyes and stared upwards.

'I – I–'

'Susan!'

'You, Douglas! I – I can't think what–'

'It's all right. You fell out of the canoe. Are you hurt?'

He put his arm about her as she sat up and shuddered. The tall man grinned and nodded several times.

'Lucky I was fishing,' he mused. 'I had a salmon nicely hooked when you came along.'

She looked at him and saw that like Tearle he was wet through.

'Did you save me?'

He nodded and turned to the younger man, who was regarding the victim of the catastrophe with undisguised admiration.

'Simpson, run down-river and see if you can get my rod. If the salmon is on it bring it too.'

Simpson, who appeared to have little hope of retrieving either, did as he was bade. Tearle held out his hand to the tall man and the latter gripped it somewhat limply.

'My name's Conway,' he informed them.

'And mine is Tearle. I'm in your debt, I guess. This lady is my wife.'

With Tearle's help Susan rose to her feet. She was pale and shaky, but appeared to have suffered no great harm from her brief immersion.

'What happened?' queried Conway in reply to her thanks.

'We shot the rapids.'

Conway opened his eyes in amazement.

'You mean you came through the chute?'

'Yes. I – I think I lost my nerve.'

'I should think so too.' He looked at Tearle. 'By Harry, you're a venturesome man to try that.'

Tearle shrugged his shoulders. There was something about Conway that aroused his instinctive dislike. Grateful as he was for the man's timely intervention, he could not choke down the innate antagonism. He ran his eyes over the mules and saw they were packed with miscellaneous survey instruments.

'Government survey?' he remarked.

'Yes. We're preparing a new map. You shall go down to immortality. I am going to label those falls Tearle Falls.'

Susan laughed amusedly. It was the first time she had laughed for so long, that it was a little humiliating to Tearle to realize that another had caused it.

'I'll go back and get the canoe along,' he remarked. 'Maybe you'd like to dry your clothes in the tent, Susan?'

'I think I would.'

Conway watched Tearle's big form disappearing along the bank. He turned to Susan with an ingratiating smile.

69

'Holiday-making, Mrs Tearle?'

'No. My husband is a trapper.'

Conway raised his eyebrows.

'And you help him?'

'Yes.' She laughed lightly. 'I am cook and general bottle-washer. We live under the skies, pitch our camp in the wilderness and forget all about that big groaning outside world.'

'It sounds very idyllic. I should like to try it myself.'

'But you are trying it!'

'Yes, with a tantalizing, unimaginative assistant like Simpson.'

It was with a sense of pleasure that Susan welcomed the break in the monotony of her existence, and the prospect of the society of other men than her husband, no matter for how brief a period. She rather hoped that Tearle would find it convenient (even while she realized that she would suggest no such thing) to make this spot a base for his expeditions.

The innuendo was a little obvious, and she frowned in order to discourage any further remarks along those lines. Nevertheless, she felt relieved to have some other man to talk to. Society in the wilderness was a pleasant enough thing.

'Are you camping here long?' she asked Conway.

'A week or so. And you?'

'I don't know. It will depend upon what kind of hunting it offers.'

'And in the winter? Your husband doesn't go after skins in the winter?'

That very matter had been worrying her. On every hand was evidenced the close approach of the winter. At nights the temperature was nearly at freezing point, and she knew that in the north-west the great cold came with startling suddenness.

'Does trapping go on through the winter?' she asked.

'Sure. I've heard of men who have spent the whole winter out in the woods, but I've never heard of a woman doing it.'

'Oh, I had no intention of staying out as long as that,' she replied. 'I – I came as a kind of holiday.'

'And you've enjoyed it?'

'Y-yes. I love the open air, the health and good feeling it brings. I've always been cramped up in cities and have never known until now the delights of the mountains, the thrills of the forests and the irresistible call to adventure.'

Though she spoke with enthusiasm he could not find any reflection of her senti-ments in her face. He wondered why, and he made up his mind to find out. When Tearle came along with the canoe a little later he pitched his tent at the far side of the clearing and built a fire outside it, and while Susan dried her clothes he talked to Conway.

'Any bear about here?'

'I've heard so.'

'Good!'

'Staying out for the winter?' remarked Conway casually.

'Yep; if I can trade the canoe for a sled.'

Conway said nothing more. He had found out a little of what he wanted to know.

CHAPTER SIX

During the next week the campers by the river saw much of each other, despite the fact that Tearle was out hunting bear all day and Conway busily engaged in surveying the north bank of the stream.

To Susan their conversation came as a vast relief from the comparative silence of the past few months. Conway was a good talker and had travelled much. The younger man, Simpson, seldom joined in, but if ever he showed a desire to do so his chief appeared to take the words out of his mouth.

'He's a bit of a fool!' explained Conway to Susan. 'The office planted him on me under the pretext that they had no other man to spare.'

'I think he is a very nice boy,' replied Susan. 'Aren't you rather hard on him?'

Conway growled under his breath. Between him and his subordinate there was little love lost, it was plain to be seen, but of course Susan or Tearle had no means of knowing the reason. Tearle on first noticing this antipathy had extended to Simpson all his sympathy.

'Still having ructions with the boss,

Simpson?' he remarked.

Simpson nodded and grinned.

'He thinks I'm no end of a mule and I think the same about him. We're quits.'

'How much longer are you going to hang about here?'

'Only a few days and then we're off to Vancouver. And you?'

Tearle shrugged his shoulders. His programme was somewhat nebulous. Had funds permitted he might have taken Susan to the coast and boarded her in some hotel for the winter. But this in the circumstances was impossible. He secretly dreaded the arrival of the cold season for reasons that were well-founded. It required little introspection on his part to realize that she was still straining at her bonds. If this was so now, to what extent must her misery be increased later?

It was this problem which had helped to bring him to other developments which had not escaped Simpson, however, and which, to some extent, accounted for his dislike for his chief. Simpson, who had observant eyes and no little imagination, was not slow to catalogue the covetous expression in Conway's eyes. Himself, admiring Susan, he had all the more reason to be inquisitive and wary.

While Tearle had been away in the woods it was not strange that Susan and Conway had become more and more friendly.

Innocent as Susan might be in the matter, though, it was not so with Conway. His eyes followed every movement of her body as they had followed another woman, an Indian girl, not so long before. Susan was not aware of this, but Simpson was. He knew the man with whom he worked, and hated him all the more for his daring. In the end, though, it was Conway himself who was the means of his own undoing. In his colossal egotism and vanity he overstepped the mark one afternoon when on the plea of having forgotten an instrument he left Simpson some two miles down the river and wandered into camp.

As he expected, Susan was alone and busily engaged in fashioning some skins into a winter garment. He was smiling as he sauntered across to her.

'Making winter garb?' he queried, and at her answering nod, he added:

'So you have decided to winter in the wilds?'

'What makes you think that?' she asked with a smile.

'Isn't it obvious?' with a wave towards the furs.

'I think not. If we go to Vancouver, I shall still require furs of some kind.'

'I suppose so,' he mused. 'But I under-stood you were not going to Vancouver. Your husband said he was staying out all through

75

the winter.'

It was difficult to ignore the challenge in his eyes or not to realize that he was aware of her own and her husband's relationship. But a feeling of resentment rose at this undisguised interest in her affairs.

'I believe that is my husband's intention,' she replied a little stiffly. 'As for me, I shall probably go to Vancouver and wait for him there.'

'You will be sorry to leave this?'

His hand waved towards the magnificent reaches of the river, but his eyes watched her face carefully.

'Wouldn't any creature with a soul be sorry to leave such a place? It gets into one's blood – the majesty of it, the great boom of the forests, the music of the river and the wild colour of the mountains.'

But, if she could deceive herself to a certain extent, she could not hoodwink Conway. Conway knew women. But clever as he was in dissecting souls he erred on the side of her pride, also in the measure of her fidelity to Tearle. For a moment he was silent.

'I know some facts are hard to face,' he said gently.

She dropped the skins into her lap and stared at him.

'What do you mean, may I ask?'

'Surely you know!' he hurried on. 'And I know you are not happy here.'

'Mr Conway, aren't you rather – indiscreet?'

A careless laugh answered her. Then he urged eagerly:

'A young and beautiful woman cannot live for long in virgin forests without such things as appeal to youth and beauty,' he said, flinging constraint to the winds.

'And what is your idea that appeals to youth and beauty?' she asked, still quietly, but the tenseness of her tone should have warned him.

'Love, romance, liberty and–'

She held up her hand imperiously and rose to her feet. Conway, who was leaning against a tree, unconsciously straightened as she stared at him indignantly.

'Exactly what are you trying to insinuate?' she asked, slowly, tensely.

'You must know!'

'That I am not happy, that I have no love, no romance in my drab life? How do you dare! You rendered me a service some time ago for which I am grateful, but that does not give you licence to intrude into my private affairs. I shall be glad if you will not speak to me again.'

Leaving him crestfallen, she walked inside her tent. Conway's hands clenched, and he swore deeply. He would have liked to believe that her annoyance, like her contentment, was assumed, but he could see it was all too real. So wounded was his vanity that immediately on Simpson's return he commenced to pack the mules for the long overdue trip down the river.

'Hooray!' exclaimed Simpson. 'It's about time we struck camp.'

'It's about time someone struck you!' growled Conway. 'Where are you going?'

'To say good-bye to Mrs Tearle.'

'There's no time. Do as you're told, damn you!'

So Simpson had to be content to wave his hand to Susan, who appeared at the door of the tent just before the mules started down the rocky path by the side of the noisy stream. She waved back and watched them disappear through the trees. Then she sighed as she realized it might be months before she saw another human being other than her husband.

It was nearing sunset when Tearle came home, and his appearance filled her with a joy she was reluctant to admit. With the memory of the past in her brain it was difficult to understand even this fleeting emotion. Was it merely admiration for his immense physique and indomitable will, or was it due to something that lived in her subconscious mind; something which her pride forbade her to give fuller expression?

She noticed that he limped as he came across the clearing from the river and wondered whether the heavy bearskin which he carried could be the cause. But when he dropped it beside the fire he stopped and rubbed his ankle with a twinge of pain.

She knew he was deliberately minimizing it, as he did all his troubles, and insisted upon examining the injury. It proved to be a nasty gash above the ankle from which the blood was issuing freely.

'Sit down and I'll bandage it,' she cried.

She knotted two handkerchiefs together and saturated them with ice-cold water from the river. When it was done he smiled and thanked her simply.

'Why have you been so long?' she asked.

'It was that bear. He led me a pretty fine dance. I found his track two miles down the river and went after him. He had the wind and knew all about me. Gee, I spent six hours getting him. Is that soup you've got there?'

He nodded towards the pot that was turning slowly round on the tripod, and she inclined her head. While she prepared the meal he hobbled down to the stream and came back with his thick hair wet and awry.

'Where's the other outfit?' he queried.

'Gone.'

'Without saying good-bye!'

'Conway seemed to be in a hurry.'

He reflected for a moment and then scanned her face, with a whimsical expression on his own.

'You'll be a trifle lonely now, I guess?'

'I suppose I shall. But eat your supper. It will get cold.'

He did as he was bade, breaking a ten-hour fast with evident enjoyment.

'Fine!' he commended, when he had finished and lighted his pipe. 'You're a good cook, Susan.'

A good cook! She wondered whether that was the utmost limit of his appreciation. He looked up as the sound of her laugh went echoing through the glades.

'What are you laughing at?'

'Oh,' Susan shrugged, 'I don't know. It occurred to me that is the first compliment you have paid me.'

'I don't think so.'

'Since we have been married I mean, of course.'

'Very likely,' he muttered. For a long time he was quiet as the smoke puffs rose in the lazy air, to aid his thoughts. Slowly then, with wrinkled brow, he asked: 'Susan, is it compliments you want?'

The question startled her by its ingenuousness. It seemed to usher in an atmosphere of familiarity that had been missing for months past.

'Any man can pay compliments,' she replied quietly. 'They cost nothing and more often than not have no basis of truth.'

'Maybe not.'

The red rays of the declining sun struck through the woodland, performing its evening miracle before the darkness came down and plunged the world into silence. Seated with her face to the west, the soft, deepening rays fell full upon her features in their repose. She saw Tearle's eyes fixed on her, and moved slightly.

'Don't!'

'What do—?'

'Don't move!' he begged. Then, after a long and alarming pause, when the last ray had vanished, 'Gee, that was wonderful!'

'What was wonderful?' she asked, wonderingly.

'The sunlight on your face,' he replied simply.

Her laughter rang out again, but it was more to cover her embarrassment than from any feeling of hilarity. Surely this big husband of hers was unlike any other man she had ever known. He could gaze at her with eyes of admiration – could speak of her beauty like this and remain as unmoved as a piece of rock. How different from the feverish glances of the man who had just gone!

'You are absurd,' she said.

He thrust his boot into the fire to spur it into a blaze and refilled his pipe. She leaned forward, and seizing a lighted brand, held it under the inverted bowl. He surveyed her calmly as the tobacco burned, and grunted his satisfaction when it was well ignited. She had never performed such an action for him before, but to-night she felt like taking this step across the chasm, for in his stolid personality she found an antidote to the bitter flavour Conway had left behind. Seated cross-legged before the blazing fire, he made a lasting impression on her sensitive brain. She felt that she was enjoying his pipe almost as much as he, as she watched the blue curled exhalations and heard his accompaniment of contented sighs.

'Tobacco,' he said at last, as though the thought of it were all his mind held. 'I reckon it's the sweetest stuff that ever grew. Here, try!'

He took the pipe from his lips, rubbed the stem of it on his sleeve, and offered it to her with an amused smile. She pursed her lips, hesitated, then took it and drew through the mouthpiece. The next instant she was coughing and rubbing her smarting eyes. He took the pipe from her trembling fingers with his left hand while his right stole round her shoulders and brought her shuddering body close to his.

The coughing ceased as she drew the pure air of the pine forests into her lungs, but the arm remained round her shoulder, for it had been extended involuntarily. When Tearle discovered it had thus wandered, he gazed at it as if it belonged to some other person than himself, and swiftly he withdrew it.

'B-better?' he quavered.

'Yes – it was horrid!'

'It is until you're used to it. But after a day's work, by the side of a camp-fire like this, there's nothing on earth more calculated to make a man thank God for life. I remember a time back in the Saskatchewan when another fellow and I went on a shooting expedition. We were six days out of anywhere when the silly mule went overboard in the canoe and two pounds of tobacco went racing down the stream. Snakes! Life wasn't the same after that. We moped round the fire at nights, cussed each other all day until that holiday was more like a riot. Then we ran into a Blackfoot Indian and he had half a pouch of mighty fierce weed. For ten cents' worth we traded over a pound of tea, two beaver skins, and a whole lot of souvenirs. But that night! It was paradise!'

From that trifling incident he wandered on to other things, to stories of sacrifice on the icebound frontiers of the Arctic, to the mad but mighty things that men do when the spirit is roused. She sat in silence, fearing to break the flow of his picturesque speech. He had the gift of bringing before her eyes the scenes of which he spoke, summing up situations in his rough way with a sparsity of words, but with startling clearness.

'Aye, if the mountains could speak you'd

hear some strange stories,' he mused.

'I'd say you do rather well yourself,' she conceded, with a nod.

'Oh, me! I can never find the right word. When you've been born and bred in the plains you can't expect to have the chin-music of a parliamentary debater.'

'Plain speech has its advantages,' replied Susan. 'It lets you know exactly where you stand.'

'Yep – that's so,' he murmured.

Something seemed suddenly to have placed a halter on his tongue. She wished he would speak again, and strove to start a conversation, but without success. She yawned and awoke him from his reverie.

'Tired?'

'Yes. I think I will go to bed.'

She stood up as did he, looking about him.

'Have you seen my blankets?' he asked.

'Yes. I took them into the tent. It rained a little this afternoon. I'll bring them to you.'

She made for the tent and he walked slowly after her. A candle was lighted within and a few moments later she came to the door with two blankets in her hand.

'Is – is that enough?'

'Sure. There's not much frost to-night.'

'It doesn't seem fair.'

'What doesn't?'

'Your sleeping out there to-night. Let me change over – just for once, please!'

He shook his head.

'Too cold.'

'You said it wasn't cold–'

'Not for me. I've slept under the stars at thirty below. It's just what one has been used to, I guess. I'd just as soon sleep outside as in.'

'You – you make me feel mean–'

'I'm sorry,' he muttered. 'I guess you took that the wrong way.'

She only handed him the blankets. He flung them across his shoulder and held out his hand with a whimsical smile.

'Good night, Susan!'

Her fingers lingered in his grasp. It surprised her that he could hold them so lightly.

'Good night, Douglas!' she murmured, and turned to go. But the touch on her fingers was no longer light. The grip increased until it almost hurt. She turned in surprise to see his face alight with conflicting emotions, and found herself being drawn within the great arms. Then in the welter of lines on his face a change came. It gathered force round the firm mouth and changed his whole aspect. She felt the grip relax.

'Good night,' he muttered, and went striding towards the fire.

CHAPTER SEVEN

Ten days more Tearle hunted in the neigh-bourhood of the camp by the river, adding considerably to his bag of pelts. Since the day of Conway's departure the relationship between Susan and her husband had bettered. She unbent a trifle. The situation became less strained and friction was reduced.

Once she went with Tearle into the hills after bear. The adventure was fruitless, but it was one she never forgot. It helped her to get a better understanding of him – to appreciate his amazing woodcraft. Through all that maze of untrodden paths Tearle picked his way with the ease and certainty of a wild animal. When it seemed to her they must be hopelessly lost Tearle never hesitated, but went plunging through the semi-darkness under the giant firs towards home with all the uncanny instinct of a bee.

'How do you know the way?' she wondered.

'Eh?'

She realized with astonishment that he did not know how he knew.

'I guess it's strange how a fellow gets to

know,' he ruminated. 'But we're hitting for the camp all right. Don't you recognize all this?'

He waved his hand about him to indicate the immediate surroundings, but to her there was nothing to distinguish them from a thousand such scenes. Each towering fir was like its brother, the thick carpet of pine needles and the undergrowth were no different from that which their feet had trod for two hours.

'It's all the same to me,' she laughed.

'Maybe you didn't take notice when we came this way.'

'Did you?'

'I reckon a man has a kind of mental reservoir which takes in and holds everything. He only has to dig down in it to find what he wants. It's darned hard work until it becomes a habit. There are a million things about trees which make every one different from the rest. Besides, there's the river. I've heard the river all the time, haven't you?'

She shook her head and marvelled at the perfection of his senses. She began to feel that after all she was only half educated, that the things she had learned at school were really of small value compared with the things which Nature had whispered to this big man. To her all this magnificence was silent. To Tearle it was full-throated and intelligible. He seemed part of it, as wild

87

and inscrutable to her as were these forest giants that reared their proud heads two hundred feet above the soil.

'There's the river,' said Tearle.

She gazed through a long avenue and caught a glimpse of silver backed by the trees on the opposite bank.

'I can hear it now,' she acquiesced.

'You could hear it all along,' he replied. 'But you didn't know it. You haven't the knack of sorting out sounds. The wind was full of them: bird cries, animal squealings, falling trees, rapids, and a thousand other things. Put a Siwash down here and he'll tell you exactly where your next-door neighbour is and what he's doing at the moment. Well, we haven't brought back much plunder!'

'I'm sorry,' she murmured. 'Perhaps it was my fault.'

'Nope. I've scared all the live things for miles around. Even a bear gets to know when a locality gets unhealthy. We'll have to hit the trail again, I reckon. Down river. Maybe I'll trade the pelts there.'

'And then?'

Susan looked at him eagerly, but quickly averted her eyes as she realized that he was scrutinizing her closely.

'Where would you like to go?' he asked quietly.

'I don't know. Why do you ask me?'

'I'd like to know.'

'Would it make any difference?'

'Maybe it would. See here, the winter is almost on us and the woods in winter are mighty bleak. There's not enough spoil for two of us to go kicking our heels in lodgings, but if prices are good for bear and beaver I'll have enough to set you down somewhere until the spring comes round.'

'And you?'

'I'll go out after something or other. Maybe I'll find a partner with enough gear to go on a big trip.'

He was waiting for her approval, but somehow she felt she wanted to reserve her opinion on the matter until she could sort out her own confused desires. Nevertheless she was grateful for the suggestion and not a little surprised that he should make it.

'I'll tell you later,' she murmured. 'I'm not sure what I want to do.'

All evening she pondered over the situation. Vancouver or some other town offered attractions, but it did not solve the problem in the least. In the spring he would come back again to claim her, unless–! She shuddered to realize where her thoughts were leading her. In the face of his solicitous attitude it seemed despicable to think of escape. She wondered if he had reckoned on that possibility, and some imp of mischief prompted her to put the question.

'If you sent me to Vancouver you'd return

in the spring?' she asked.

'Sure!'

'Suppose – suppose I had gone?'

'Where?'

'Anywhere – home.'

He shrugged his big shoulders as he wrestled with a bundle of pelts.

'You haven't the means,' he grunted.

'But I could escape – anywhere. In offering me this you are putting temptation in my way. Hadn't you thought of that?'

'Not much. There was no need.'

'Why not?'

'You couldn't get far. I guess I'd find you all right.'

His composure was like an icy hand on her heart. She had hoped for something else; some expression of trust or sign of anger at the reminder. Anything would have been better than this unnatural calm and the faith he had in his ability to hitch her to his chariot whenever he pleased.

And so was a new rift created. Between them the past persisted in rearing its ugly head. Good intentions were misconstrued on either side, and war once more took the place of peace. That night she went to her tent without even the customary handshake. But it hurt her perhaps more than it did him, for bad feeling could not root over a certain seed in her bosom. In her consciousness she called him tyrant and heartless monster, but the queer whispering went on within all the same.

The next morning they struck camp and started down the river westward. The canoe was heavily laden with pelts and gear, and care had to be exercised to prevent it swamping. In the bright but cold autumn sunshine they were borne on the tumbling water, through rapids and rocks in a veritable fairyland of nature. The keen air and the thrill of rapid movement had the effect of banishing discord, at least for the time being.

'Where to?' asked Susan.

'To a township of some kind. I've got scarcely any ammunition left and food's mightily low. Sit more amidships!'

For two hours the pleasant voyage continued. The scene changed; the saw-tooth mountains moved round to the north, the river widened and the gaunt red rock all but disappeared from the banks. The trees were more magnificent than any she had seen before and ran to the edge of the water on either shore. They passed a tributary which was belching millions of gallons of mountain water into the parent stream, and were swung by the fierce current to the opposite bank.

'Drive her inshore!' yelled Tearle. 'I saw—'

She did not hear the end of the sentence, but drove in the paddle almost horizontally and saw the craft leap the breakers and move into the more placid water close to the bank. She looked round to see Tearle ramming a cartridge into his rifle.

'Keep her nose in,' he cried. 'I saw a grizzly just now.'

The bow entered the shallows and Tearle hastily leapt ashore and scrambled up the bank. Susan, not to be left out of so thrilling a sport, pulled the canoe close to the bank by means of the paddle, and slipping the mooring line rather carelessly round a tree, scrambled over the boulders and up the steep incline. She trod lightly in Tearle's tracks, but a full ten minutes elapsed before she overtook him to find him leaning across a rock with the rifle in the crook of his arm.

'Douglas!' she whispered.

He turned his head quickly.

'I came to see you get him.'

'No luck!' he muttered. 'I've lost him.'

'Too bad!'

They waited for some time, but the bear did not again appear; Tearle rose and slung the rifle over his shoulder.

'He's away by now. Have to get back.'

They made their way through the trees and down to the river bank. From the ledge above the stream Tearle looked down and uttered a low cry.

'What's the matter?' asked Susan.

'The canoe! Where did you leave the canoe?'

'There – tied to a tree. Can't you see it?'

She craned her neck forward and saw the tree to which the craft had been moored, but it was not there.

'Gone!' she ejaculated.

'Did you fix it in the way I showed you?'

'I – I don't think I did. I was in a hurry. But surely it can't have gone far?'

Tearle set his mouth grimly as he gazed downstream. Near the centre the current ran at a good eight knots. He could see down the banks for half a mile but there was no sign of the craft. It was evident it had slipped its moorings and had drifted in the main current.

'Is – is it lost?' stammered Susan.

'Yep. It's miles downstream by this time and making for the sea for all its worth.'

'But our food, our tent, and the skins!'

'All gone. Hell!' he muttered.

Her heart beat furiously as she reflected upon the calamity and what it meant to them. In the canoe were the results of three months' hard labour. All gone because she had been too hurried to fashion a secure knot. Tears welled to her eyes as she became conscious of her own responsibility in the matter.

'Douglas, I–'

'No use wailing about it,' he said calmly. 'We're landed and we've got to make the best of it.'

'But it was all my fault. I ought not to have left the canoe.'

'You ought not.'

'Oh–!'

Tears streamed down her face. His equanimity seemed to make matters worse. She felt he should have gone into a violent fit of temper in the circumstances. Had he beaten her she would have taken it as her due.

'Don't cry,' he said. 'We're still alive and kicking.'

'But we've no food!'

'We'll get some.'

'And the skins! They were worth a thousand dollars! You said so.'

'Maybe I was exaggerating.'

'Why – why do you belittle this?' she retorted. 'You know we are in a terrible position. Even if we strike some township we shall be penniless.'

'So,' he replied. 'But I guess we'll pull through. I wish I had kept that map in my pocket, though.'

'Are we near a settlement?'

'Can't remember. Let's be beating it. We're wasting time.'

She gulped and dabbed her eyes with her pocket handkerchief, then followed him down the river bank. Hours passed and the river continued to thread its way through the forest. When the sun had reached its zenith Tearle stopped and sat down on a tree-bole.

'Hungry?' he queried.

'Not very,' she quavered.

'I guess that ain't true. Say, have you got a pin of any kind?'

Wonderingly she found a safety-pin and handed it to him. With a few twists of his muscular fingers he fashioned it into a hook and, producing a ball of twine from his pocket, attached the hook to the end of it. A piece of bark from a neighbouring tree served as a float, and a few minutes later was turning round and round in the water some ten yards from the bank with a large worm on the hook.

'It won't hold anything bigger'n a two-pounder,' commented Tearle. 'But we won't grumble at that.'

His patience was extraordinary. Three times he lost his worm and had to probe about in the earth for another, and once he got a fine fish out of the water only to lose it before it could be landed. But in the end he won, and a denizen of the river was safely brought to the bank.

Tearle's method of cookery was primitive but satisfactory. He lighted a fire and then hunted for a flat piece of rock. On this improvised frying-pan the fish spluttered and sizzled, exuding an odour calculated to tickle the palate of one who, like Susan, had waited for two solid hours for the result. Together they finished the fish, eating it as savages might, with their fingers.

They went on again until the sun sank in the west and the air grew chilly. Tearle tried the fish-line again and had the bad luck to lose the hook. He gazed at the end of the twine ruefully.

'Any more pins?'

'N-no.'

That night was Susan's first introduction to unsatisfied hunger, and the feeling was not pleasant. Fortunately Tearle still possessed a few matches, and the presence of a blazing fire drove off some of the other discomforts.

'Maybe I'll shoot something in the morning,' said Tearle.

She nodded, her heart too full for words. He left her for some time and came back with both arms full of pine branches, from which he made a not uncomfortable bed for her. She noticed that his own portion of branches was small and commented on it.

'Got to watch the fire,' he explained. 'There's only two matches left and I guess we'll want those before we finish. You make yourself comfortable.'

She reclined on the branches and gazed across at him as he sat cross-legged before the blaze, smoking serenely. Even now, after three months of close contact with him, he was a stranger to her. She could not reach below the rugged exterior with any certainty of finding the real man. Pondering his complex personality, she fell asleep, and it was not until daybreak that she opened her tired eyes. He was still beside the fire, sitting in exactly the same attitude as if he had not moved a single inch during the night, and to her amazement his arms were bare. She rubbed her eyes and then discovered that his coat was spread over her.

'Hello, Susan!'

She started at the deep voice and clutched at the garment over her.

'G-good morning! Why did you take off your coat?' she demanded.

'I kinder felt warm,' he replied calmly. 'Better yank it over. I'll put it on and go after something for breakfast.'

CHAPTER EIGHT

For three, long, tiring days Tearle and Susan tramped down the river. Every hour saw an increase of width from bank to bank and a slackening of the current. On the afternoon of the third day it was no longer a river but a lake measuring some two miles at its greatest width and apparently narrowing again further down.

About ninety miles had been covered since the loss of the canoe, and in all that distance they had met no habitation of any kind. One meal a day had been their fare, first the fish and then a large bird which Tearle had brought down with his last cartridge, the latter serving for two meals.

How Susan had kept going she did not know. There were times when she felt like giving up and facing the grim consequences of such a step, but Tearle always seemed to be aware of the approach of these crises and fired her flagging optimism once more by a cheery remark. In the face of such an example she could not do other than continue on the weary march, trusting in his strength and will-power to pull her through.

'Bound to hit on a settlement soon,' he

said. 'This ain't Central Africa.'

An hour later he stopped and inclined his head towards the wind. She scarcely noticed the halt or the action, for her own head was aching and half her senses dulled. Only when Tearle uttered a little hiss did she realize that something was exciting him. She looked at him wistfully.

'Did you hear that?' he half whispered.

'I heard nothing.'

'It was a falling fir.'

'Well?'

'Not the tree that falls of its own accord. I guess that one was well notched! There – listen!'

She turned her head to the wind and thought she heard a queer dull thudding mingled with a metallic twang.

'What is it?'

'Loggers at work.'

'Loggers?'

'Timber-jacks. That's the ring of the axe and the buzz of the saw. The other noise was the earth-quiver when a two-hundred-foot stick comes toppling. I've heard those noises too many times to be mistaken.'

They proceeded along the lake at a quicker pace. The thuds and other noises grew more distinct, and occasionally above them came the shrill note of a whistle.

'Donkey-engine,' informed Tearle. 'We'll see the camp soon and a sea of stumps. Gee, this is luck!'

Ten minutes later they rounded a bend and came within view of the camp. It lay about fifty yards from the edge of the lake, a few scattered wooden buildings mingled with tents and apparatus, looking like a box of toys in comparison with the giant trees in the background. Stretching away to the right of the camp for a distance of half a mile or so were massive stumps neatly shorn a few feet above the basal swelling. Beyond them the loggers were at work with axe and saw with the rattling, quivering donkey-engine hauling at full pressure.

'Timber!'

The human cry came simultaneously with a cracking somewhere in the sky. The air became full of a weird whistling and swishing and then a mighty crash as a monarch of the forest came to earth, beating into pulp the smaller things which stood in its path.

'He's down,' exulted Tearle. 'Can you smell the sap and the resin?'

Susan could. It permeated the whole atmosphere. Coming from out of the silence this sudden change to hideous noise and titanic energy was overwhelming. Among the trees and fallen logs she could see scores of shirted men moving about, and axes and saws gleaming. It was like a war with Nature in which the human animal was winning all the time. But they did not win without casualties, for as they moved forward a man emerged from the forest with his arm roughly bandaged and blood dripping from an unseen wound. Their line of progress intersected his and Tearle stopped him.

'Messed up?' he queried.

The big bearded fellow showed a set of yellow teeth.

'Splinter. That big stick flipped up some small stuff. Where did you hike from?'

'Down the river. Where's the boss?'

'He's running the engine – the donkey-engineer's gone sick.'

The bandage on his arm grew completely saturated. He gazed at it calmly and then inclined his head down the lake.

'Got a doc down on the steamer. He'll put something on this.'

He turned abruptly and went swinging through the stumps whistling as if the six-inch wound in his arm were nothing. Susan shuddered.

'These fellows are sure hard,' said Tearle. 'You get like it when you handle big stuff. I'm going to see the boss. You sit down and rest.'

She nodded and watched him stride across to the noisy donkey-engine on which stood a greasy, smoke-begrimed figure, naked to the waist and looking more fearful than the gang he ran. In all her life she had never seen such men as these. They seemed apart from the common run of humanity, a race of atavistic monsters, all bone and muscle, with faces which defied analysis. She reflected that her husband was very similar and equally large and dominating.

The man at the donkey-engine saw Tearle waiting, but he was too busy watching the manoeuvring of a massive log into the clear to pay any attention to strangers. When at last the fifty-foot piece was on the brim of the chute ready to be bunted into the lake he mopped his brow and turned to the stranger.

'What you want?'

'Graft.'

'What kin you tackle!'

'Anything going. I'll run this old engine if you'll step down.'

'You could?'

'Sure!'

'All right – run it!'

Tearle slipped off his coat and displayed two long bulging arms and a breadth of shoulder which took the eye of the 'boss.' His gaze wandered up the big figure.

'What do you tip the scale at?' he growled.

'A pound over two hundred.'

'All that, I guess.' He watched Tearle operating the donkey and nodded his head as he realized he was fit for the job. 'You'll do. I'll put you on the pay-roll. What name?'

'Tearle – Dug Tearle.'

He made a rough note on the back of an envelope which he took from his breeches pocket, and then suddenly noticed Susan in the background.

'Hell! You didn't tell me you'd brought your harem.'

Tearle's brow clouded at the remark, for by the quick movement of Susan's hands he guessed she had overheard it.

'She comes in, too,' he growled. 'You can take it out of me in extra graft.'

'You ain't going to be capable of anything over and above what I'm going to knock outer you before I'm through,' retorted the 'boss.' He reflected a moment and then turned his fierce black eyes towards the waiting woman. 'Got room for a woman in the cook-house,' he barked. 'Can she cook?'

'I should smile! Hi, Susan!'

She came slowly across to them, striving to choke down the resentment she felt at being referred to with about as much respect as one might use on the donkey-engine.

'We're hired,' said Tearle with a whimsical little smile.

'We!'

'Yep, you in the cook-house, me on this jigger. Does it go?'

She was on the verge of screaming 'No' when she caught Tearle's eyes. In them was a challenge she could not refuse, a mute appeal to her common sense and her capacity for endurance. It aroused within her the determination to see the thing through, to prove to him that she was something more than a bundle of curls and dimples.

'It's a bargain,' she replied in a low voice.

Then the privations and sufferings of the past few days overcame her resistance, and she swayed and clutched at the stump of a tree. Tearle left the donkey and sprang across to her.

'Hold up!' he muttered. 'It's food you want.' He turned to the boss. 'I'll come back in a few minutes. Where's that grub shop?'

'The squat shack along there. You needn't come back to-night; it's knocking-off time. I'll send a feller across with you to show you round. Hi, Rafferty!'

A man who was working on the edge of the clearing looked up and flung down his double-bitted axe. He came through the brush wiping his face with a great red handkerchief.

'What's wrong, Shag?' he asked.

Shag – short for Shaggin – explained in a few terse words, and Rafferty stuck a plug of tobacco in his back teeth and nodded. He leered at Tearle and kept his eyes averted from Susan as if she were something to steer clear of.

'Foller me!' he muttered.

The cook-house was almost as noisy as the donkey-engine, despite the fact that only two persons were in it. One was a rather pretty French half-breed girl, and the other a placid Chinaman in sagging blue overalls. The infernal din was created by the handling of a hundred or two enamel mugs and plates which Nicotte, the girl, was flinging down a long table to be caught deftly by the Chinaman at the other end. When Rafferty and Tearle entered, followed by the amazed and nervous Susan, the noise ceased, and Nicotte gazed in wonderment at the visitors, from which spell Rafferty aroused her by spitting on the floor.

'Mon Dieu!' she gasped. 'I keel you one day!'

'Let up!' growled Rafferty. 'Here's a guy and a – a lady wanting grub. Shag told me to put some pep into the establishment. Here Foo, move that corpse of yours and hustle up some eats.'

Foo caught a hurtling enamelled plate dexterously, and stood with it spinning on his upturned finger, a bland smile on his moonlike face.

'Ain't he a beaut!' muttered Rafferty. 'Used to run a conjuring outfit down at Vancouver. What are you staring at?'

This to Nicotte, who was lost in admiration of Susan, much to the latter's embarrassment. The French girl moved with a start and in a few minutes had spread an enormous meal at one end of the table. Rafferty, having made sure that everything was in order, lounged towards the door.

'Got to get a bunk fixed up,' he explained. 'But Susan's sure got me guessing. Can't doss in the bunk-house, that's sartin–'

Susan nearly choked at the free use of her Christian name, but Tearle seemed unperturbed, and Nicotte, watching them furtively from the other side of the room, displayed no astonishment. Rafferty scratched his head in perplexity and went out. Susan glanced at her husband, who was calmly eating his way through the big meal.

'Are all lumber camps like this?' she asked.

'Much the same. Maybe it'll shock you a bit at first but you'll get used to it.'

'And what is the bunk-house? You – you're going there?'

'Looks like it.'

'And I?'

'I'll fix you up,' he replied, then touching her arm almost tenderly, 'there's nothing disgraceful or lowering in honest work, I guess. You'll hear hard words spoken here and they'll call you Susan, and treat you like a sister. That's the way of the lumber-jack. He's hard as the stuff he wrestles with, but you treat him as a man and an equal and there's nothing he won't do to keep your respect.'

She nodded silently and turned her eyes towards the figure of the dark Nicotte, who crossed the room to them with lithe movements of her young slim body, dis-

106

playing a perfect set of pearl-white teeth.

'Maybe you lak me git you hot water for wash, yes?'

'Thank you,' murmured Susan. 'I should be glad.'

A few minutes later Nicotte returned to announce that the water was ready. Susan followed her into a diminutive room at the far end of the hut. It was like Nicotte herself; a mystery room, full of quaint things, from an Indian headdress to several beautifully marked snake-skins nailed on the wall. On an improvised dressing-table stood a looking-glass, brushes and comb, and some feminine requisites. At the head of the trestle bed was a washstand with a tin basin.

The wash and brush-up refreshed Susan. She was putting the last touch to her hair when Nicotte came back. Through the mirror she saw the girl's oval face filled with such evident admiration that she blushed to reflect that she was the object of it.

'Feenish?' queried the girl.

'Yes, thank you.'

'I jus' see Shag. He say you come to help in cook-house?'

Susan nodded a bit nervously, wondering in what light Nicotte would regard this intrusion.

'Shag say you help cook?' she repeated, questioningly.

'I am going to try.'

'Foo cook dam' bad. Maybe you teach Foo somet'ing, yes?'

Susan laughed at the quaint English, and the eyes of Nicotte blazed as for a moment she thought she was being ridiculed, but the next moment they were soft again and she laughed in crooning fashion.

'I t'ink I lak you,' she said. 'Maybe you try and lak me a leetle, yes?'

'I'm sure I shall,' replied Susan warmly. 'Nicotte, is my husband still outside?'

Nicotte opened her eyes wide.

'That beeg man – he your husband?'

'Yes, what did you think?'

Nicotte shrugged her shoulders in silence, but what she had thought was so obvious that Susan could not mistake it. A little later she found Tearle lounging at the door of the cook-house.

'I've fixed it,' he informed. 'Luckily that infernal bunk-house was packed as full as a sardine tin. Shag has had to fall back on a shack at the far end of the camp which has fallen out of use. He's putting in a couple of shake-downs and some odds and ends. We'll do fine there.'

In her heart she was mightily glad. In this camp on the fringe of the vast forest she felt completely at sea. The people who moved and had their being amid the big timber were not the people of her world. Tearle was like them in many ways, she thought, but at least she knew something of him, and the desire to be near him at times was surely natural.

While Tearle was assisting in getting her future home in order, Susan talked with Nicotte. The dark-skinned girl interested and fascinated her. She was in many ways the counterpart of the loggers, quick to passionate anger and possessed of a pride which was manifest in every line of her body. Being as she had been, up to now the only woman in camp, did not embarrass her in the least. She met these rough men on their own footing and won for herself as much respect as any woman could wring from any man in a civilized community.

'Zay are jus' zee leetle child at heart,' she murmured. 'Las' month I have a birthday and Shag he send all down to Vancouver a beeg list of beau-tiful t'ings. Each man he buy one and write my name on it and put it beside zee plate after supper. Zat night I kees zem all.'

It was impossible to resist her charm. Susan thanked God there was at least one woman in the fierce community when circumstances made it necessary for her to live there for some time. To Nicotte her sympathy and friendship were already being directed. It afforded some outlet to a full heart that was feeling the strain of pent-up emotion.

The shack assigned them, as Susan found, was a small affair but clean, and it boasted a stove in the centre of the living-room, by the side of which was piled a high stack of pine logs. She noticed that the floor was still damp.

'Did they scrub it?' she queried.

'I had a go at it,' confessed Tearle, then hurriedly: 'It'll dry before morning if we keep the stove fired.'

There seemed to be no limit to the man's capacity for work! Tearle hunting huge bear in the mountains! Tearle on hands and knees scrubbing floors! Could anything be more incongruous!

He walked across the room and opened a door. Inside was a bedroom, also scrubbed and clean, with an iron bedstead in the corner and a table beside it.

'Yours,' he said. 'You've got a fine view of the lake. There's another bedroom next to it, through that door. It's a mighty silly arrangement because I shall have to come through this room to get to mine. But maybe in a day or two I can nail up this door and cut another way through to the kitchen.'

'Does – does it matter?' she hesitated.

'Sure! They rise mighty early in a logger camp. I'd be bursting through when you were in bed. You leave it to me. I'll fix it!'

She tried to feel grateful for this

considerate treatment, but somehow it rankled. What a chance to drag down the barrier and how reluctant he was to accept it! She thought she hated him for his pugnacity and yet he had been good to her in his own queer fashion. But to nail up a door—

CHAPTER NINE

Life in the lumber camp was like being a cog in a whirling, devastating machine. At first Susan found it interesting enough, but the novelty soon wore off. One day came to be much like another, and once she was acquainted with the round of work she grew tired of the monotony of it.

But the human element retained its interest. The men who sawed and hacked at the giant firs were queer customers. Their capacity for toil was as enormous as was their capacity for food when the mighty battle of the day was over and the great logs lay stretched on the ground or were bunted into the insatiable lake for rafting down the river.

Shaggin drove his crew unmercifully. He was on a big contract – millions of feet of timber – and nothing would satisfy him but to see it worked out to schedule. Above the screeching of the saws the thudding of his booming voice rose, bawling orders or cursing as the circumstances ordained.

When Susan had time to spare she would go to the scene of destruction and watch the silent agonies of the forest. She saw that

Shaggin made full use of the competitive spirit. First went the sawyers to the selected trees, wedging a spring-board into a horizontal slit in the base of the doomed giant. Seated on the two ends of this they plied the keen saw until the proud monarch of the forest dipped his head before the ignominious crash which sealed his doom. It fell almost exactly on the spot designated by the fellers who had previously notched it on the line of the saw mark, and who leapt from their perches at the warning, ominous creak.

Followed, the gang whose job it was to dismember the branches. On their heels came those who sliced the long length into handier sections ready for the indefatigable donkey to haul into the clearing and down the chute into the lake.

Shaggin worked his different gangs in such nicety of proportion and strength that no part of it ever managed to overtake another. It was part of his strategy to offer the swampers and buckers fifty dollars to catch up with the sawyers. The sawyers in their turn were duly apprised of the plot and out of pride determined to thwart it. So Shaggin accelerated the process of destruction.

'The way to get a full day's work from a fellow is to touch him on his soft place,' he once said to Susan.

'First of all one must find the soft spot,'

113

laughed Susan, who found it difficult to believe that these hardbaked sons of the forest had anything soft about them.

'Pride,' growled Shaggin. 'Maybe it's jungle pride, but it's rooted there as deep as those firs. They're proud of their strength and of what they can do with axe and saw. Listen to their talk; it's all consarned with logs, or maybe with fighting. Fight! By gosh, if those fellows got fighting there'd be hell to pay.'

'I hope they won't,' said Susan, soberly.

Shaggin laughed and shook his head.

'I only had 'em scrapping once,' he confessed. 'Some dirty Siwash ran up the river with two gallons of whisky. It was inside. Gee, this part of the country hummed for twenty hours. But keep 'em away from booze and a quieter lot never breathed.'

He turned his eyes towards the grimy slaving figure of Tearle on the donkey-engine.

'Give me a gang of workers like that and I'd change this old earth. He's ten horse power.'

Susan said nothing, believing the remark an invitation to discuss her husband. In a way she liked and admired Shaggin, but he had an unpleasant knack of intruding. That he liked Tearle was clear, but he overstepped the mark in assuming that the growing friendship between himself and his donkey-engineer gave him licence to intrude into personal

114

matters. Shaggin had looked in at the shack by the lake and he had not failed to notice the nailed-up door and the new entrance to Tearle's bedroom from the kitchen. That unusual state of affairs exercised his mind considerably.

'Dug's a dark horse,' he mused.

'What do you mean?'

'Got something on his mind.'

'Nonsense!'

'Ain't you noticed that?' he asked pointedly.

'I see so little of him,' she murmured.

This was true now. Tearle spent little of his time in the shack. To her chagrin he seemed to find the company of his mates preferable to her own. When the work of the day was over she invariably went to the shack to find him away, either gambling in the bunkhouse or gossiping amiably with Nicotte.

She could not fail to notice the difference in his attitude to Nicotte and to herself. With the pretty half-caste girl he would chat and laugh for an hour on end; to his wife, he was merely polite and attentive. How the change had come about she could not think, but imagined it was due to the different environment. Before they had struck the lumber camp they had been comrades, 'trail mates,' as Tearle called it. Now the machine had gobbled them both up. They were but cogs in this noisy thing. Their individuality seemed to have been sunk in it. Inwardly, she pined for release both from the monotony of it and from the thankless toil of the cook-house.

She reflected that she had dropped her pride, had left behind all the niceties of life for no reward other than the knowledge that she was earning her food. What could she see in Tearle's attitude but callous indifference cloaked by an exterior politeness which hurt even more than a brutal expression?

And Tearle! Tearle flirted with the pretty Nicotte to try to forget that his wife had one night talked in her sleep. He had been going to bed late, when he heard a cry from behind the thin partition. A little apprehensive he had opened the door and held the lamp above his head. She was lying with half the bed-clothes dragged off her as if her dreams were troublesome. He was about to close the door when she murmured:

'First you've got to find a wealthy husband – it's a crazy scheme – yes, I'll do it if it kills me. Peg – we can't give up this – bills, bills–!'

It had brought back the past in vivid perspective. He saw himself again the poor duped fool. Had he stayed a little longer he might have heard pathetic additions to the rambling talk, but the punishing toil of the day had left him tired and impatient. He went to his room with bitterness at his heart and let it soak in deeply.

Nicotte amused him in the same way that gambling amused him, for he was given neither to flirting nor gambling, normally. It was easier to talk with Nicotte than with Susan. Between them there was no terrible past to obtrude and wound. And Nicotte with all her passionate nature stirred, was wondering – wondering.

Tearle came home late one evening to find Susan sitting over the stove in an attitude of deep thought. She started up as he closed the door with a bang.

'You – you frightened me!'

'Nerves, nerves. You mustn't get nervy.'

'Is it snowing?' was her only response, as she noticed the flakes on his shoulders.

'Yep; she's come at last.'

'Will it stop work?'

'Not much. Shag's working out his contract. Gee, we broke records to-day. By the way, that fellow never pulled through,' he commented, as he shook the flakes from his heavy cap before hanging it up behind the door.

'What fellow?'

'The sawyer who got in the way of a falling fir. Didn't you hear about it?'

Susan shuddered and shook her head. Such incidents were rare. Men got gashed and bruised with splinters and stones, but as a rule the sawyers were miraculously efficient in dropping a tree and knew just where and when to jump.

'Never recovered consciousness. Poor devil!' added Tearle, drawing his chair up before the fire.

'It's horrible!'

'It's life; it's work.'

'I know, but it's horrible to think about. I want to get away from here! I can't stand it any longer! We seem to have shut out life for ever. There's no pleasure, no joy here. It's all toil – toil – toil – from sunrise to sunset.'

'You mustn't buck at toil. It brings bread.'

'Yes, but I'm human. I want the things I'm missing. I want–'

She stopped as she felt his eyes fixed on her.

'Well, what is it you want?' he asked, with a slow calm.

'Something – anything! Here there is nothing. Douglas, when are we going to leave? It isn't Vancouver I want. Take me out on the trail – into the mountains, but take me, take me before I go mad!'

Never had he seen her so agitated. It puzzled him because he could see no good cause for it. He could not know that her heart was yearning for a fuller expression of an emotion which had been born in the wilderness. One thing he saw clearly. She was almost on the verge of a nervous

118

breakdown. His expression changed as his naturally sympathetic nature overrode his smouldering antagonism.

'We'll get away then, Susan,' he promised.

'You mean it?'

'Sure! I guess this camp is a pretty stifling place to a town-bred woman. I'll see Shag to-morrow and hand in my notice.'

Her relief was overwhelming. She had never imagined that the time would come when she would welcome with open arms the winding trail, the solitudes of winter in the wilds, but compared to the camp it seemed paradise. Since they had been there they had had no heart-to-heart talks; no camp-fire stories such as had to-night brought them closer together. Out there among the snowclad hills there was no other woman to exercise a fascination over him. He would be hers, and hers alone, to walk with, talk with, suffer with.

She flushed to reflect that Nicotte should creep into these considerations, for her pride forbade her to admit that Nicotte mattered much. But there it was in her subconsciousness and it was already assuming large proportions.

But Tearle's plans were cancelled by an unexpected happening. When the gong was beaten at six o'clock next morning by Shaggin himself, not more than half the loggers turned out, and some of these wore strange and ominous expressions. Tearle was firing up the donkey-engine when Shaggin appeared with a savage scowl on his face. He looked at Tearle keenly.

'Morning!' cried Tearle. 'The snow was light after all.'

'So you're all right?' grunted Shaggin.

'All right? I don't get you.'

'It's here.'

'What's here?'

'Booze. Someone has got it across and I'm going to find out who it was. There's half the crew lying dead drunk in the bunk-house and the other half ain't fit for graft.'

He swung round on his heel as a sawyer approached with unsteady gait.

'Hello, Shag!' he hiccoughed. 'This is damn fine weather for felling trees.'

He lurched towards Shaggin, and his shoulders were gripped by the boss logger's huge hands.

'Where'd you get it?'

'Eh?'

'Talk up, you whisky-soaked chunk of hard-bake. Who handed that stuff out to you?'

The sawyer let loose a growl and gathered himself together. Suddenly he shook off Shaggin's grip and hit out with his fist. It caught his employer on the side of the head and sent him staggering. The gauge for battle was down, and Shaggin was not the man to refuse it. He was bigger than his opponent and as hard as nails. The drunken man made a futile attempt to defend himself, but in less than a minute he was gasping in the snow and bleeding profusely. Shaggin, beside himself with rage, strode across to the bunk-house. What happened there Tearle did not know, but he heard the uproar that came from the building, and a few minutes later a crowd of fighting figures emerged.

Tearle immediately left the engine and ran across. When he arrived on the scene, Shaggin was in combat with three men. His coat and shirt were torn from his back, and all over his body were the marks of cruel punishment. He saw Tearle coming and waved him back.

'Don't start anything, Dug,' he yelled. 'I can finish this all right.'

That his optimism was not justified was proven when Rafferty, who had just received a terrific blow in the face and was mad with drink and pain, stooped and lifted a huge block of wood and flung it with a savage curse. It hit Shaggin on the hip full force, and sent him to earth with a groan. His effort to rise was valiant, but it failed and he lay with face convulsed. It was more than Tearle could stand. He leapt at Rafferty.

'Come on,' he growled, punctuating his challenge with a blow that told. 'I'm taking this over for a spell!'

And on they came. But in Tearle they found an antagonist even better equipped than the last. Shaggin had been merely powerful, but Tearle was that, and more. He had science and youth on his side added to the deep anger engendered by Rafferty's foul blow.

For ten minutes the battle raged. The less drunken of the men came from the clearing and were content to watch, making wagers among themselves as to the outcome. Susan, who had heard the fracas from the shack, appeared on the scene just as Tearle was finishing off the second man. She stood aghast at the awful sight, but noticing the prone figure of Shaggin, ran to him.

Tearle dashed at the third man, seized him in his arms and with a Herculean effort threw him bodily down the chute and into the lake. A growl of deep admiration came from the watching men. Even the two beaten men on the ground joined in. This kind of thing appealed to them as nothing else could. Rafferty, much sobered, lurched across.

'By gosh, you're my money. Put it there!'

'You're a low-down skunk, Rafferty, and you're fired.'

'Fired? Who the–!'

Tearle pointed down the lake.

'I'll give you half an hour to beat it out of

camp. If you stay longer I'll give you a dose to remember!'

Without waiting to hear what objections Rafferty might have he returned and went to Shaggin, who was without doubt in great pain, but still tried to smile at him.

'Gee, you're great, Dug,' he painfully complimented, his words coming wheezingly. 'I'm out of action for a bit. Get me down to the steamer before it leaves, will you? I'll have to lie up before I'm through. That donkey-engineer will be back to-day. Dug, will you take over until I'm well? You're the only man here to run this crew.'

'I'm sorry–' demurred Tearle.

'You can't go back on me, Dug,' pleaded Shaggin. 'You see how it is with them. If they ain't beaten to it they'll be swilling that stuff again. Do this for me and I'll make it right. Maybe I'll have to go to Vancouver, but you bet your life I'll soon be whooping up here again. Say, will you do it?'

For a moment only Tearle hesitated, then slowly he inclined his head.

CHAPTER TEN

The steamer left the lake the next morning with Shaggin on board, and Tearle found himself temporarily in charge of the camp. The mutinous section of the men turned up for work again, but they were a little sullen, as if they resented this sudden promotion of Tearle to the position of boss logger.

Tearle, however, fell into his new job as easily as he had suppressed the fight. Acting on his former decision he had sent Rafferty out of camp after a terse lecture on fair play. Work proceeded amid the wonderful transformation of the new snow. It lay like powdered salt over everything, blinding in its unmarred whiteness, and falling in glistening cascades from the laden branches as the vibrations of axe and saw and falling trees released it.

The old donkey-engineer, a square-headed Irish-American named Logan, took up his duties, and the general working of the camp went on without halt. But Tearle was on the alert for the reappearance of the cause of the recent trouble – whisky. It came two days after Shaggin's departure. He was sitting in Shaggin's office shortly after work had ceased for the day when he saw an Indian beaching a canoe along the bank. Simultaneously a man left the bunk-house opposite and wandered through the trees.

Tearle set his jaws and, picking up a revolver, left the office. From the cover of a tree he saw the Indian take a gallon jug from the canoe and place it on the ground while he bargained with the man who had apparently expected him. Tearle saw a roll of bills change hands. The logger was stooping to pick up the jug when Tearle raised the revolver and fired.

The bullet hit the jar square and shattered it to fragments. The Indian jumped aside, but the logger stood as if petrified as he watched a gallon of whisky trickling into the lake.

'So that's how it gets here?' came a growl, and Tearle, striding into the opening, towered over the culprits.

More quickly than he drew it, the Indian put back his knife as he saw the barrel of Tearle's revolver moved up. The logger's lips moved and his eyes blazed hate.

'Get into the canoe,' ordered Tearle.

'What the–!'

'Get into the canoe! Your redskin friend can take you where you want to go.'

'I'll see you in hell first.'

Tearle moved forward to shove the nose of the revolver into the man's side.

'Beat it!'

'There's fifty dollars owing me,' he complained sullenly.

Tearle managed to extract the amount from his pocket, and, crushing the notes into a ball, flung them into the canoe, without once lowering his weapon.

'You took this job on conditions,' Tearle told him sternly, 'and you've broken them. I've no use for guys who start trouble in camp. If you or this Siwash land on this shore again I'll shoot at sight. Sheer off!'

Muttering vengeance, the man climbed into the canoe and the Indian followed. Tearle watched them making across the lake, and he hoped he would see them no more. When he arrived at the office Susan was waiting for him, her face a trifle pale.

'I thought I heard a shot fired,' she said.

'You did. I've just put a stop to a whisky deal.'

'You – you haven't shot – anyone?' she gasped.

'Nope. The whisky was the only victim. Did you want anything?'

She hesitated for a moment as if the question embarrassed her considerably.

'I – you didn't come home last night. Nicotte said she brought your breakfast in here.'

'That's so,' he replied calmly. 'I'm taking over Shag's hut. It's more convenient. There

126

are papers and things I have to attend to.'

'I see,' she murmured.

But she didn't in the least see why the change should be necessary. The other shack was less than a quarter of a mile away. Any bookkeeping could be done there just as easily. And there was Nicotte. Because Nicotte had always looked after Shaggin's requirements, was it essential that she should do the same for his successor?

Tearle could see his wife was angry, but he under-estimated the depth of her emotion, believing it due to the enforced stay at the camp.

'I shall have to carry on until Shaggin returns,' he explained. 'I gave him my word.'

'You also gave *me* your word,' she retorted, then more bitterly, 'I might have known better! It is not the first time you've given me your word.'

He flushed as memory gave meaning to his wife's words, and there was a little sharpness in the apology he tendered.

'I know, but I guess circumstances forced me to go back on it. It was hard to have to do that, Susan.'

Only her shrugged shoulders answered him.

'You don't believe it?'

'What am I to believe! First it was yourself, now you put Shaggin above me. You consider this business of timber, timber,

127

timber, far more important than – than my happiness.'

'You're taking a wrong view of things, as you've done before,' he growled. 'Would you have me refuse to give a man a hand when he is down?'

'Shaggin's not down. This makes no difference to him. Though he works like any logger he's rich. All he thinks about is dollars and timber and contracts. He is unable to conceive anything better in the world than this grubbing for profits, and nigger-driving. I hate the whole business. I loathe the grease and the smell, the noise and the foul language. Don't you realize this is soul-murder to any woman?'

She hesitated a moment, searching for the control her passionate outburst had taken from her.

'Nicotte seems to have survived it,' was Tearle's calm retort.

'Nicotte!' She laughed bitterly. At such a moment as this he could drag in the name of Nicotte, the girl who was now waiting on him, obviously admiring him, perhaps even falling in love with him!

'I'm surprised you should mention her,' she said, with a kind of sneer she could not conceal.

Tearle's eyes flashed ominously.

'Why the hell shouldn't I?' he barked.

She put her hands to her ears.

'Can't you speak without swearing now? Is that the language you use to Nicotte?'

'Susan! What's got you?'

'Nothing has got me. It's you! You have become just like the others, brutalized, indifferent to anything but slavery, and – and Nicotte.'

As she swung round she caught sight of a small handkerchief on the floor. It was marked with a large 'N' and was one of a dozen given to Nicotte by Shaggin on her last birthday. Susan held it with the tips of her fingers as she dropped it on the desk before her husband.

'Eau de Cologne,' she said. 'Nicotte's chief attraction. She must have dropped it in her agitation.'

Tearle made no effort to speak to, or stop her as she swept through the door. He was hurt. For he had spoken truly when he regretted his inability to fulfil his promise to Susan. He had remembered it when Shaggin begged him to take over control of the camp, but felt that under the circumstances she would understand and uphold his decision. Even now he failed to realize where the shoe pinched. Her references to Nicotte were pointed enough, but his innocence was so complete he refused to take them seriously.

He hung into a pile of clerical work connected with the business of the camp, and which was much in arrears, but his mind was far away. Susan was not the kind of woman to be banished like a puff of smoke. Deeper and deeper became the impress she created on his heart and brain, and only his stubborn spirit prevented him from acknowledging it. He could not forget that she had acted a part with consummate skill less than six months ago. Was it not highly probable she was acting now? The subtle advances she made towards a reconciliation, the wistful glances, the simulation of jealousy. What were these but snares to outwit him?

The maddening desire to respond to her was only checked by keeping green the memory of the past. That was his sure rock of defence to which he meant to cling. Nicotte. He laughed grimly as he thought how insignificant was the pretty half-breed girl in comparison with a woman of Susan's presence, beauty, and culture. Nicotte was merely charming, a delightful daughter of the wild and the friend of all the world. Susan was more than that. Susan in the cook-house with her sleeves rolled up was still the queen.

He realized that the work was going badly. He could not concentrate on it. The columns of figures danced before his eyes and grew confused, meaningless. He pushed the ledger away and lighted a pipe, gazing wistfully through the window into the gloaming. A few minutes later there was a noise behind him. He turned and saw Nicotte, her head and shoulders covered with snow.

'I make up zee fire,' she lisped. 'It ees ver' cold.'

He swung round in the chair and watched her push a dozen big logs into the stove. She closed the door with her foot and began to tidy up the room, humming lightly as she did so.

'Is it snowing again, Nicotte?'

'Oui. I t'ink a big blizzard he come soon. Maybe he stop zee work heer.'

'Maybe he won't,' laughed Tearle. 'We aren't stopping for anything on earth. There's another hundred thousand feet of timber wanted before anyone in this camp takes a holiday.'

'Zen you go away, yes?'

'What makes you think that?'

Nicotte laughed strangely; then she was silent for a moment. She came closer and looked at him furtively.

'I t'ink you stay too long heer.'

Tearle put out his hand and grasped her arm, causing her averted face to come round.

'Now what do you mean by that, Nicotte?'

'Nussing.'

'You must mean something. Speak up –

you needn't be afraid.'

Nicotte had some difficulty in meeting his steady eyes. She had always that difficulty, for Tearle had made a strong impression on her sensitive heart and quick imagination. No other man had impressed her in this way. The loggers were different. She regarded them as brothers, and in their company was very much like themselves. For years she had abandoned her sex, slowly acquiring masculinity. Now Tearle had awakened something that was as discomfiting as it was exciting. Her heart wanted it to continue, but her reason rang a warning note in her brain.

'Someone want you very much,' she murmured.

'Someone– Who?'

'Sacré! But you are blind!'

Tearle shut his mouth like a trap. It annoyed him a little that this girl should probe into his personal drama, even though she took, as he believed, a wrong view of the situation.

'Now you are ver' angry,' she mused. 'I hate for to make you angry, mon ami.'

The deep and sincere regret in her voice, the tremulous eyelids, the heaving bosom moved him. But still he did not realize that what was emanating from her whole being was passionate love, controlled only by power of will. He saw only a pure friendship untainted by any other element, and he wanted nothing better – from her. He raised her hand to his lips and kissed it.

'I won't get mad with you, Nicotte. You're making a thundering big mistake, because there are things you don't know. But I reckon your advice is nickel-plated. Gee, you were right about a blizzard!'

Wind struck the building in fury, and a whirling mass of fine snow hit up against the window. From outside came the eerie boom of the giant firs, and then above that a rending crash and a trembling of the earth.

'Mon Dieu!' gasped Nicotte.

He clutched her trembling body in his arms and heard a queer little sigh from her lips.

'Only an old fir – the big fellow near the bunk-house. We ought to have had him down before. He was rotten and dangerous.'

The door burst open and through it plunged a white figure which halted at the sight of Tearle and Nicotte in an attitude much like an embrace. Tearle stared at the intruder as Nicotte drew back. It was Conway, the surveyor.

'Sorry to burst in like this,' he panted. 'We got caught in the blizzard – lost our tent and had to beat it down the river. I saw a light and thought it was Shaggin's place.'

'It was,' grunted Tearle. 'But Shaggin's away. Shut the door or I'll lose all my furniture!'

Conway went to the door through which the snow was beating and called, 'Simp – where are you?' A voice answered, and a few seconds later Simpson came into view with the two mules in tow.

'What about these darned animals?' he cried.

'There's a shed behind,' replied Tearle. 'Here, I'll show you.'

He jammed on a cap and went out to help Simpson in getting the two miserable mules under cover. When he returned with the boy Conway was sitting by the stove talking to Nicotte. He rose as Tearle entered, and Tearle was conscious his grin held a meaning.

'This damn job will be the death of me,' he complained. 'I've still got to survey this side of the lake before I can make tracks to civilization. Can you give us a shakedown?'

Tearle reflected. The bunk-house was full and every tent he possessed was occupied.

'You'd better have this place,' he offered, as he remembered Susan's shack was the only available place.

'Hang it, I can't very well turn you–'

'You needn't worry. I can find a shake-down.'

'Well, it's mighty considerate of you, old chap. Quite a coincidence running across you again!'

'Quite!' replied Tearle shortly.

134

'And Mrs Tearle; is she here?'

Tearle nodded and started to gather together the things he needed to take with him. Simpson, who was thawing his half-frozen hands, seemed curiously reflective. Conway's remark amazed him because both he and his chief knew quite well that Tearle was running the camp and that Susan was with him. That information they had from Rafferty, whom they had run across the day before. He began to wonder whether the blizzard had not come at a favourable moment for Conway, and whether the tent had not been assisted in its flight. But like a wise youth he said nothing.

A meal was served for them later by Nicotte, and they took up their temporary quarters while Tearle plunged through the driving snow to inhabit his recently abandoned room. Susan's first intimation of the change was the entry of Tearle amid a cloud of snow.

'I've come back,' he said.

'So I see.'

Casual though her remark, she was obviously waiting for an explanation. Tearle shook the snow from his shoulders, and sat down near the stove.

'Some old acquaintances have turned up,' he said. 'That surveyor fellow and his assistant.'

'Mr Conway!'

135

'Yep. Got caught in the storm and lost their tent. I had to find room for them.'

'Of course!'

If he looked for any sign of any effect his news might have caused he was disappointed, for Susan's only move was but a flicker of her eyelids.

CHAPTER ELEVEN

The storm passed and left the woods knee-deep in snow. But that small fact was no deterrent to Tearle in his zest to work out the contract before Shaggin returned. At break of day out went the loggers to battle with the giants. From dawn till chilly eve the noise of axe and saw filled the woods and the logs splashed through the thin ice into the lake.

If Conway really had work to do in the neighbourhood it appeared to occupy but a small amount of his time. His greeting from Susan was somewhat chilly, for she still remembered their parting and was not quick to forgive him. But as the days went on she was surprised to realize she was getting some pleasure from his society.

Tearle was far too busy to worry about his temporary guests. If he noticed they existed at all it was only to the extent of a nod at a distance. The loggers themselves regarded the two surveyors as outside their world, and went about their work and pleasure with their customary thoroughness.

So it was that Conway and Susan were flung together and in that reunited acquaintanceship Conway found his old hunger for her aroused. He was wise enough not to display an inkling of his inner feelings, nor to exhibit any interest whatsoever in the affairs of Susan and her husband, though circumstances were operating in his favour, and he was content to wait his opportunity; to gain his end by other means than a headlong rush into forbidden territory.

The exact relationship between Tearle and Nicotte he did not know. True he had seen the girl practically in Tearle's arms on his entry to the camp, but succeeding events did not warrant his deducting any important fact from that. Intuitively he divined that on Tearle's side there was nothing but friendship. But Nicotte was different. There was more than friendship there. He saw it in her glances at Susan, and in Susan's chilly attitude in response. To be certain he dropped a few pointed remarks to Nicotte, and was met with a blaze of wrath.

'I'm sorry,' he said. 'It was merely a jest.'

'I hate your jests,' she stormed. 'By gar, I t'ink you very bad man.'

'Really, you took it too seriously.'

'I do not lak you, no. You are too much like zee panther. You prowl, prowl, prowl and you watch everyt'ing. For why you watch so?'

He passed it off in an amused laugh, but

he was convinced that no help could be expected in that direction. It was obvious to him that Nicotte did not wish her love affair to be helped out by anyone – that she knew it was hopeless and wanted to keep it hidden in the depths of her warm and innocent heart.

'She's a strange girl,' he said to Susan.

'I see nothing strange in her.'

'Then you are more unobservant than I imagined. I think she hates everyone but your husband.'

She glanced at him swiftly, but his face was composed and she was obliged to take the remark as casual.

'You're wrong,' she replied calmly. 'Nicotte has no hate. She is merely impetuous. She speaks the first thing that comes to her lips; the first thing.'

He was not deceived. She was trying to excuse Nicotte against her own convictions. She was not anxious for him to know of the friction which existed between her and the girl lest he should draw obvious con-clusions. He laughed lightly.

'She certainly dislikes me, whatever you may say. I invariably manage to stroke her the wrong way. When I leave camp she'll utter a huge sigh of relief.'

'So will you, I expect.'

'Why should I?'

'You told me once you were dying to get

back to civilization. Have you changed your mind?'

'Yes,' he replied softly.

'Why?'

'The greatest thing in life is congenial company. Vancouver cannot offer anything better than I am getting here. But I suppose I shall have to go,' he added ruefully.

'Of course you will.'

'Perhaps you and your husband will give me the opportunity to pay you back if ever you come to Vancouver?'

'Pay us back? What for?'

'For your kindness in letting me use the camp as headquarters.'

'You must thank Shaggin,' she said. 'He's the real host. My husband is only filling a gap until he returns.'

'And then you'll start off again on your travels. By Jove, I envy Tearle!'

His tone was so sincere she laughed.

'Susan!'

It pulled her up with a jerk and her wide eyes stared at him in astonishment.

'Really, you mustn't–'

'But everybody here calls you Susan.'

'They're different. It's their regular form of address. They know nothing of common civility. They called Shaggin "Shag" or Bill.'

'But Susan's a delightful name!'

'That has nothing to do with it.'

'And a delightful person,' he added.

140

She held up her hand and then pointed to the dimly seen figure of Tearle standing on a gigantic log bellowing to his toiling crew.

'Only my husband may say that.'

'Oh, he wouldn't object – if you didn't,' he laughed, and his shoulders lifted.

'Why do you think that?' asked Susan sharply.

'Far too busy elsewhere.'

In the man's face was something which lent the words sinister meaning.

'What do you mean?' she half whispered.

'Too much work. He works far too hard. You ought to force him to take a rest.'

The explanation failed to carry conviction, just as he intended it. It put an end to their conversation, too, but it left him feeling that he had made progress. Nothing more was needed but an occasional subtle reminder that her faithfulness was being wasted.

The weather grew colder, and a bleak wind prevailed for several days with intermittent snow, which clogged the forest and made work a terrible thing. But still Tearle had his men out to time and inspired them by the force of example.

'Boys,' he cried, 'we've got records nailed down fast. It'll sure make Shaggin jump when he looks at the hole we've driven. I guess there's never been anything like it since those big sticks first threw out roots.'

All the men's antipathy was gone now. Tearle was the 'goods.' Tearle could twist them round his finger. Logan, the Irish donkey-man, confided to some of his mates that the boss-logger was only half Canadian, and that the other half was Irish.

'Where can ye find a man loike thot onywhere out of Ireland? Glory be! have ye seen the arms and legs of him? I only knew wan man fit to walk beside him, and he was born in my native village o' Ballymaroon.'

The patriotic outburst brought a cry of dissension from a big Californian, the biggest man in camp and one of the quietest. Logan's constant praise of the green isle got on his nerves, and he spoke more with the object of getting one back at the Irishman than in praise of his own strength.

'You and your Irish,' he growled. 'The boss has no more Irish blood in him than that darn tree. As for arms, what about these?'

He bent his two enormous arms so that the muscles bulged beneath the skin. They were prodigious – the result of handling big things for a score of years. But Logan, loath to confess to an exaggeration, shook his head.

'It's mesilf who'll back the boss against any wan of ye at a trial of strength. I'll lay a week's wages on him I will and all.'

Nothing was so calculated to start a general argument. The men were divided in their opinions. The Californian was certainly the bigger man, but Tearle was the younger. They began to make side-bets on a contest.

'Let up!' growled the Californian. 'Tearle won't stand for any horse-play.'

'Sure he will,' retorted Logan. 'I'll ask him.'

When he did, Tearle, by dint of subtle arguments on Logan's part, was cajoled into settling a score of bets. He turned up at the bunk-house on the following afternoon, which was a half-holiday, and slapped the Californian on the shoulder.

'What's all this nonsense, Mat?'

'It's not my doing,' growled Mat. 'Logan wants to see us kill each other.'

'Only wan need get kilt,' retorted Logan. 'And I know who it'll be.'

A roar of laughter greeted the sally, and the two prospective opponents realized that any withdrawal would mean bitter disappointment, so agreed to carry out the programme. By general consent a wrestling match was agreed upon, and a large ring was cleared of snow.

The combat which followed was terrific. The camp was as noisy as a circus. Half an hour passed and still no result was obtained. Susan, brought from the shack by the din, stood on the outside of the ring and frowned, horrified. To her the thing seemed beastly; appalling. For a long time she failed to realize that it was merely play; that even under the fierce 'holds' the two big men bore each other no ill-feeling.

Conway stood beside her, on his face a strange smile. Whatever the outcome might be he cared not. His own enjoyment was derived from Susan's obvious displeasure. But even Susan was not bereft of the sporting instinct. A magnificent effort of Tearle's brought a roar of applause from the crowd. To her own amazement she found herself participating in it. Her enthusiasm once aroused, it rose higher and higher. The frown left her face and her eyes followed every movement of the supple bodies.

'Go on Douglas!' she cried.

Then she met Conway's eyes, and what she saw there brought a sense of shame. She wanted to get away from the place; to forget that she could have shown interest in so brutal a scene. And yet, within her was exultant admiration for her husband's strength and vitality.

A terrific outburst brought her to realize that it was all over. Tearle was sitting across Mat's big chest pulling at his beard playfully. Then he held out his hand and helped the Californian to his feet.

'Hooray!' yelled Logan. 'Didn't I tell ye so!'

144

Mat mopped his brow with one hand and extended the other to his victor.

'You're sure the toughest guy I've ever laid hands on,' he growled. 'I guess it's youth that done it.'

'No! It was just trickery, Mat. You had the beef, but I had the tricks. Here, where's my coat? I ought to be working.'

He made his way through the excited crowd and halted by the side of Susan. She smiled at him and took the coat from under his arm, holding it out that he might put it on. Then she left Conway, and went with Tearle back to the shack.

'Why did you do it?' she asked.

'They wanted it. It amused them, and they deserve a little amusement. Are you annoyed?'

'I – I don't know,' she stammered. 'I – I think I should have been more annoyed if he had won.'

Her loyalty surprised him a little, coming as it did after days of silence.

'It's curious how this sort of thing counts with them,' he mused. 'If I had more brain and less muscle I wouldn't get the same results. You have to apply different methods to different conditions. I'd be a rank failure in a big city.'

'I don't think you'd be a failure – anywhere.'

'You're wrong. Wasn't I down and out in

145

London? A fellow belongs to the place that bred him – and a woman too, maybe,' he added half-acknowledgingly.

'Even a woman may change.'

He wished he knew exactly what she meant, but he would not ask. Believing that Shaggin must return in a few days, he was reluctant to widen the gulf between them by reviving the past. Unknown to her he was planning for an early departure from the camp, hoping that the future might do something to mend the rupture.

Though matters were progressing so satis-factorily for the purpose Conway had in mind, they were still too slow for his time limit. He realized he must help them along. At best he and Simpson could find no excuse for a more protracted stay at the camp. Moreover, what was the use? Any day might see the return of Shaggin, and that undoubtedly meant that Susan and her husband would take to the trail again, and down once more would go the house of cards the surveyor had been so carefully building.

Conway was uneasy, too, where Simpson was concerned. He knew, only too well, that Simpson was aware of his purpose, and was watching him. And he knew, also, that Simpson knew him too well to be deceived by any masquerade. Despise Simpson as he might, he was compelled to credit him with this much. It behoved him, therefore, to move as warily, and swiftly, as possible.

When chance played into his hands, like the quick-witted knave he was, he took advantage of it. After leaving the scene of the wrestling-match he wandered across to the lake to think. Despite the snow and the sharp nip in the air, the rays of the sun were pleasantly warm, and Nicotte was sitting outside her quarters complacently darning stockings, as he passed. She looked up as he approached and nodded somewhat coldly.

'Still annoyed with me, Nicotte?' he asked with a grin.

'I am only annoyed with you when you make me angry.'

'Well, I won't do it again. Am I forgiven?'

'I do not know. I will see how you behave in future, yes.'

'I'm afraid you won't have a chance. I am leaving tomorrow.'

'I am ver' sorry.'

'You are not. On the contrary, you are relieved. Eh?'

'Maybe,' she replied. 'Why I cook for you who do no work? For days and days you do nussing but prowl, prowl–'

'Doubtless you would like to see me squatting on one of those ridiculous perches pushing a saw through five feet of timber.'

'It would be ver' good for you.'

147

'Perhaps. But I prefer being a long distance from where those big things fall.'

He picked up one of the darned stockings and gazed at the mended part in admiration. 'You're an expert with–'

She snatched it from him quickly, and put it into her lap with half a dozen others. Conway laughed easily, and raising his cap went down to the lake. His little problem was solved. He thought he saw a way to bring about the crisis he had in view. It rested with nothing more important than a pair of stockings.

He hung about until he saw Nicotte get up from the chair and enter the cook-house. Then she came out with a scarf around her head and hurried off. The man waited until she was out of sight, and then stole round the hut. When he went back to his own shack a few minutes later, there was a pair of Nicotte's brown stockings in his pocket.

CHAPTER TWELVE

'So you are really leaving to-morrow?'

Simpson nodded his head, and gazed down the ice-rimmed river as if he already saw the buildings of Vancouver in the distance.

'Did you get a tent?' Susan continued, interested.

'Yes, the chief dug one up from somewhere. It'll be a wretched journey, I guess, without a sled. We could make one easily in a couple of days, but now Conway is just as keen to get away as he was to stay a few days back. I can't understand him.'

'You've finished your work then?'

'Yes. We could have gone long ago if we had hustled. Of all the creeping snails!'

She laughed amusedly at his undisguised antipathy to his chief, but ascribed it to professional jealousy.

'Cheer up,' she murmured. 'You'll soon be home again.'

'Jolly good thing too. It's the rottenest trip I've ever made. We've done nothing but wrangle the whole time. Shall you be staying here long?'

'I don't know. It was a chance for my

husband to make some money, and it was necessary for us–'

'Of course. But didn't the hunting pay well?'

She bit her lips at the recollection of the catastrophe which had resulted in so much loss.

'We lost all our skins,' she explained. 'I was careless and let the canoe drift away with all it held – our food, clothes, tent, everything.'

He opened his eyes sympathetically.

'My! that was bad luck, but I guess Tearle will put things straight. I wish it had been my luck to work with a fellow like Tearle instead of– Oh, well, what's the use of flying off the handle? I suppose even Conway has some use in the world.'

'Mr Simpson,' she remonstrated. 'Aren't you just a little unjust?'

'Not a bit. Why pretend I like him when I don't? Of course *you* see him in a different light. He managed to save your life up the river, and that is bound to count. Bit of luck for him. Wish it had been me.'

'It shall be your turn – next time, I promise,' she laughed.

His natural good humour returned, and he chatted with her for a while longer. Then in the distance he saw Conway waving his hand at him.

'Wants me to lend a hand packing,' he remarked. 'We'll be hitting the trail immediately after breakfast.'

She watched him bounding across the snow in the roseate light of the afterglow. A glance at the watch which she wore on her wrist caused her to hurry towards the cook-house to help Foo in preparing the men's supper. The odour of fried fish was wafted across to her as she approached the place and the lilt of a queer song which Foo always sang when he cooked fish. He had told her solemnly and seriously it was an incantation to the souls of the dead fishes, expressive of his woe at thus treating them.

Five minutes later she was immersed in the work she hated. Had it been for Tearle alone she might have got some satisfaction out of it, but to cook for a tribe was vastly different. The sickening smell, the heat, the heavy atmosphere in the airless kitchen, the drone of voices from the room where the men ate, the clash and rattle of plates – her soul revolted against it all.

On going into the dining-room, she discovered that Nicotte was not there. Fearful that the meal would be late she left Foo to the cooking, and commenced to lay the long table with plates and knives and forks. She was finishing, when her glance wandered to the window. Coming across the snow in the queer half-darkness were Nicotte and Tearle. She heard the latter's deep laughter ring out as they neared the place and it hurt her like a stab from a knife.

Nicotte entered alone, her face flushed with the keen evening air and her eyes bright. She halted as she saw the laid table and the waiting figure of Susan.

'T'ank you,' she lisped. 'That is ver' good of you.'

'Have you had a pleasant walk?'

'Y-es. I meet zee boss on zee way back. He–'

Susan laughed, and the face of Nicotte went crimson. Her hands clenched, and she glared.

'Why you laugh?' she demanded, trembling with rage.

'I was merely thinking how fortunate you were to meet my husband – on the way back.'

Before Nicotte, in her wrath, could find a fitting retort, Susan had marched through the door. There was scant time for quarrelling then. The hungry army strolled in and Nicotte was kept busy for over an hour.

Susan made her way to her shack as soon as the meal was over. She felt sick and weary of it all. If this slavery led to any good result, she would have been contented enough. But to toil and suffer while her husband flirted about with a half-breed girl! Her anger was too deep to permit reasoning. Her starved heart was fast growing as cold as the stars that hung like lamps over the camp.

She heard Tearle coming, but in her

present mood was not anxious to see him. A quarrel that would serve no purpose would undoubtedly be the outcome. Before he could open the outer door she had retreated to her bedroom. She heard the door bang and after a brief pause a knock sounded on her own door.

'Susan!'

'What's the matter?'

'Have you gone to bed?'

'Yes.'

'There's nothing wrong with you, is there?'

'No, I'm tired, that's all.'

She heard no more from him, nor did she expect to, for his pride would prevent him from begging her to come out and talk. She crept into bed, but found sleep a difficult matter. Before her half-conscious brain swam the vision of Nicotte, the innocent-looking Nicotte, who she felt convinced was slowly taking Tearle from her.

The next morning found Conway busy completing his packing. The two mules were tethered to the stump of a tree outside the office and Simpson was checking an inventory of their possessions.

'All correct?' queried Conway.

'Yep, but we'll want some more canned beef.'

'Run over to the store and trade a few tins.'

Simpson made across the snow just as Susan came into view. She stopped him and glanced towards the waiting mules.

'Ready to go?'

'Yes, but we're short of grub. I'm going to trade some. Is Tearle about?'

She shook her head and his face fell.

'I would have liked to say good-bye. Will he be long?'

'I don't know. He went out early this morning through the woods.'

'Perhaps we'll meet him on the way.'

'I don't think you will. He went in the other direction. He delights in long walks on Sunday as a relief from the work of the week. Is Mr Conway inside?'

As she spoke Conway came outside and added another bundle to a mule's pack. He nodded towards Susan, and she walked across to him.

'You're away early,' she remarked.

'I hope to be. I'm only waiting for some more provisions. The weather doesn't look too promising.'

'How long will it take?'

'Six days. It's a beautiful trip.'

'It must be,' she sighed. 'I think I have developed into a nomad since I came out here. I feel the insistent call of the trail. I almost wish I were coming.'

'Why not?' he laughed. 'That lazy Chinaman can do the cooking without your help.

154

Nicotte could give him a hand. She seems to spend a great deal of her time gadding about.'

She frowned at the mention of Nicotte, and he was tactful enough not to mention her again.

'I'll go and see Tearle and persuade him to let you come back with us to Vancouver. Simpson is an excellent chaperon.'

She shook her head and laughed.

'My husband has gone out for the day, searching for big trees.'

He smiled to himself and looked to see if Simpson was coming, but the boy was not in sight.

'By the way, I found something belonging to you,' he said suddenly. 'I all but packed it with my blankets.'

'Something belonging to me!'

'Yes. You'll never guess.'

'I certainly cannot. Where did you find it?'

He pointed to the office.

'Then it doesn't belong to me, because I have never been in there – at least only once – and I am certain I left nothing behind. What is it?'

He went to the window, slipped his arm inside and brought forth a roll of hosiery.

'Perhaps I ought not to have said anything – about – them,' he stammered. 'I'm – I'm sorry.'

She held the stockings in her hand bereft

155

of speech. The thing was so utterly un-expected it produced a temporary paralysis. Conway simulated an expression of bewilderment.

'I'm sorry,' he muttered. 'I didn't mean to be impertinent. I–'

'Where did you find these?' she stammered.

'Under the mattress of my bed – er – at least Tearle's bed. I put some maps there the night I came and– But what is the matter?'

'Nothing,' she breathed, but he smiled at her painful effort when she tried to force a smile as she noticed a big hole in the heel of one of the stockings. 'It's time that was mended.'

She gave no thought to Conway or what he might think. Her brain was whirling. The discovery was significant enough to obliterate trifles. Afraid to face him longer with such thoughts hammering at her brain, she held out her hand.

'Good-bye. I hope you will have a pleasant journey.'

He retained her hand and gazed into her face keenly. Her simulated composure was transparent enough to him. Beneath it all he saw horror, and anger, and desperation.

'You seem perturbed,' he muttered.

'Nonsense! I–'

Then he let his eyes fall on the stockings and uttered a little ejaculation of astonishment, as though to convey the fact that something had just occurred to him. It was admirably acted, and created just the effect intended on the unsuspecting Susan.

'By heaven!' he muttered. 'I never thought of that!'

'What are you saying?' she asked dully, as though not comprehending.

'I just remembered you said you had only been inside that place on one occasion. If that is so—'

'I made a mistake.'

'Are you sure?'

'Y-es.' Then violently: 'How dare you question me? Let me go!'

As he released her hand, she was off like a streak with no backward glance. Conway watched her go with a gleam of triumph in his eyes. The carefully acted plot had succeeded so far. Not yet was the curtain rung down, but he believed it would not be long. She could not – would not – question Tearle, and the same outraged pride would prevent her from demanding an explanation from Nicotte.

Susan, reaching the shack, flung herself on the bed, and at last came the tears of anguish. She had recognized the stockings as Nicotte's. Explanations! What explanation was necessary? The presence of the damning things taken into conjunction with other incidents, all vividly revived now, could only lead to one conclusion.

And that conclusion was hideous. Whatever Tearle might be otherwise, she had believed him incapable of such a thing as appeared incontrovertible. Was this why he had been so keen to occupy Shaggin's quarters? And he was the man who had nailed up the door communicating between her room and his own. Her bitter laugh hurt her more than tears. Anger was no antidote to the soul-shattering consciousness of the truth.

She dried her eyes, and strove to face the thing bravely. Since Tearle himself had seen fit to bring about this final crash, she could do no more than accept the cruel challenge. To fight for him, to attempt to win him from another woman's arms, was a humiliation nothing would persuade her to face.

She looked through the window, and saw Conway and Simpson with the two mules wending their way across the snow. The thing that had been in the back of her mind many times before, in a flash became an obsession. Escape! And here was the means literally at her door.

Conway, anticipating the emotions which swept her, was hanging behind the struggling animals waiting for some sign from the woman he had tricked. He was within a hundred yards of the door when Susan came out and beckoned him. Simpson walking ahead saw and heard nothing. Conway

158

stopped as though surprised, and lifted his brows interrogatively.

'Mr Conway–' hesitated Susan, but just for the space of a second, then she went on with determination. 'Will – will you take me to Vancouver?'

'Now?'

'Yes – yes. But don't ask me anything.'

'I will do anything you ask.'

'Then wait for me farther down. I will join you in ten minutes behind that clump of firs.'

She pointed down the lake and he followed her finger, and nodded silently. The next minute he was making after the mules and the ignorant Simpson.

Susan went inside to pack the few things she would require. It took no more than a few minutes for she possessed little more than what she stood in. Then came the problem of what to say to Tearle. She tried to scribble a message, but the words came with difficulty, and she tore it up. After all, was there any need to explain anything? The reason must be clear to his guilty conscience.

She decided to write nothing, but noticing the stockings on the chair beside her she picked them up, and with a murmur of disgust placed them in the centre of the table. Then slinging her bundle over her shoulder, she wrapped the scarf tightly round her throat and made off down the lake.

CHAPTER THIRTEEN

It *was* late in the afternoon when Tearle returned to camp. He emerged from the woods near the lake and made his way straight to the shack. To his astonishment the fire was nearly out and the temperature inside the place almost as low as it was in the open. He flung off the snow-boots which he was wearing and banked up the stove with logs from the wood-pile.

In half an hour the stove was almost red-hot and the kettle on the top of it was boiling merrily. He went to the cupboard and hunted up a packet of tea and other articles of food, for he was ravenous from his long walk.

That Susan was absent did not surprise him. Of late she had appeared deliberately to avoid him on every possible occasion. It was true that only yesterday she had unbent slightly, but he was reluctant to draw any hasty conclusions from that. The promise which circumstances had made it impossible for him to fulfil caused him no little self-reproach. His one desire now was for Shaggin's return so that he might take Susan away from this place which she had hated so much.

He was fast coming to realize that her misery and antagonism did not leave him unaffected. Though he strove to find comfort and forgetfulness in work, it was a palpable failure. With Susan about him there was no forgetfulness. She was not the kind to be forgotten. This woman who he still believed had tricked him into marriage, who had aroused within him the flames of fierce anger, had aroused something else as well, and it had come to be an ache that would not be effaced.

He was spreading the tea things on the table, when he noticed the pair of brown stockings. Whether Susan wore blue, black or brown stockings, he had never noticed. He had always thought of her as a personality without regard to dress. That they were her stockings he had not the slightest doubt, though why she should leave them in the centre of the table, he made no attempt to guess. He picked them up and dropped them on a chair by the window.

He was hoping she would come in soon, for the place seemed dull without her. Though she only sat there in her customary silence it were better than being without her. The consciousness of his hope made him frown. Why, in the face of all that had happened, did he wish this? He was nothing to her – nothing. Even that sinister surveyor with the tongue of a serpent was more important in her eyes. Many times he had seen her laughing with him – laughing!

She had pleaded for the trail again. Was that merely a clever subterfuge to lead him into thinking wild impossible things? In this shack their relationship was of an unnatural kind. Could it be any different out there in the wilderness where they would see each other every minute of the day?

He thought not. And yet things had not always been so bad as they were now. There had been times when the light of gladness had flashed in her eyes. There had been occasions when a curious sigh had fallen from his lips. They had been strangers even then, but the estrangement had not had this bitter sting about it.

The fact was, he had failed. He was forced to that conclusion by all the evidence before him. He had set out to break her, to make her pay the full price of her duplicity. He had achieved nothing but bitter failure; deep wounds self-inflicted. What was there left but to bury the ruthless axe and set her free?

That was what he meant to do when Shaggin returned. It was six days down to Vancouver. He wished it might be six hours that the end might be reached the quicker. He reckoned he would have enough funds to buy her a passage to England, and thus

162

write *finis* to an adventure such as he never dreamed would happen to him.

After that – well, after that the future lay entirely with their separate inclinations. For him there was always this free life of the woods and the mountains. For her there remained her youth and her beauty, not to mention her art.

A knock on the door aroused him from his reflections. A second later Nicotte's head came round the corner. The dark eyes searched the room and finally rested on him.

'Come in, Nicotte,' he said.

'I look for Susan,' she murmured. 'Foo want her ver' much.'

'Foo will have to wait. She's out.'

'But zee supper – he will be late. Where she go? – look for her.'

'I don't know where she is. I have been out all day. She may have gone along the lake with Mr Conway or Mr Simpson.'

Nicotte opened her eyes wide.

'But zay are gone.'

'Gone?'

'Zay leave ziss morning.'

'Conway told me he was leaving to-morrow. Are you sure?'

'*Mais oui.* I say goodbye to heem. He look for you but you are not heer.'

'Well then, Susan must have gone for a walk alone. Probably you will find her when

163

you get back. Did–'

He stopped as he saw Nicotte's eyes widen as they focused themselves on the pair of brown stockings under the window. She crept across and picked them up.

'What you do with my stockings?' she asked, with a blush.

'Your stockings?'

'I lose them yesterday.'

'You must have left them here.'

'No, I not come here yesterday.'

Tearle spread out his hands.

'Anyway there they are. You'd better take them away, Nicotte.'

She rolled them into a ball and thrust them into the pocket of the short beaver coat which she wore. The expression on her face puzzled him.

'What's the matter?' he asked.

'Nussing – nussing.'

'But–!'

'Oh, you are so silly,' she retorted. 'Why you take my stockings and leave them heer?'

Tearle glared at her, but the next moment he laughed.

'Taking ladies' stockings ain't one of my recreations,' he said. 'What's got you, kid?'

Nicotte so nearly choked that without another word she went through the door, leaving Tearle perplexed. But the incident next moment passed off as too trivial for thought.

When he had finished his lonely meal, he began to make up his accounts ready to hand over to Shaggin on his return. It was two hours later that Nicotte returned, her face pale and her lips trembling.

'Is Susan heer?' she quavered.

'Nope. Didn't she go over to the cook-house?'

She shook her head and stared hard at him. There was something in the stare to cause a chill to run down the man's spine. He rose and put his hand on her shoulder.

'Nicotte, are you guessing things?' he came to the point.

'No, no – but–'

'But what?'

'I not see Susan since ziss morning.'

'Well, what then?'

She recoiled before the blazing eyes. She knew that he knew what was in her mind, but confronted with that angry challenge she felt mean and speechless.

'Go back,' he growled and sat down heavily in the chair.

She crept to the door and hesitated there.

'You are angry with Nicotte because–'

'Because what?' he hissed.

'Mon Dieu, you are mad – mad! You will not see – you will not see!'

She closed the door behind her and vanished.

Tearle sat like a statue for a few minutes.

165

At last it was all plain to him – what had happened, but strangely enough, as is so often the case in great crises, it was not the numbing big thing that was for the moment uppermost, but, in his case, a childish irritability with Nicotte. What in hell had she been waiting for, expecting, anyhow? For him to make some noisy demonstration; wave his hands about like a lunatic and call down hell and destruction on everyone? That Susan had gone was clear enough, but he could not bring himself to believe she had gone with Conway. That was what really mattered.

He flung open the door of her room and found that her few belongings were no longer there. He looked round for some message which might help to make things clearer, but he found none. Then he lighted a lantern and putting on a coat went out of the shack to examine the footprints. Outside the door the snow was beaten flat, but a short distance away the tracks separated. He found Nicotte's leading across to the cookhouse. Crossing these were other tracks that led towards the side of the lake. Following them he came upon the unmistakable imprint of the mules' feet. Then he found the place by a clump of firs where the mules had apparently waited, for the snow was kicked about; pawed.

The smaller impressions he traced back

again to the shack. It was all plain enough. Conway had waited for Susan to join him at the clump of firs. At that point she had mounted one of the mules, for beyond it there were but two sets of footprints, Conway's and Simpson's.

Back in the shack he sat down to ponder the situation. Despite the glaring facts of the case he refused to see anything more than the putting into practice a threat many times expressed – escape from him and the monotonous life of the camp. Conway merely represented a channel of escape; an escort, for Simpson was there, too, and at least Simpson was straight.

Nevertheless the thing rankled deep within him. He had promised to take her away once Shaggin returned. Why had she not waited? Then there came visions of Conway with his subtle, smirking smile. It sent the hot blood flowing through his brain. However much he might excuse her, however much he might attempt to crush the microbe of suspicion, this was a challenge not easily ignored. He imagined her beating down the trail under the guardianship of the man he detested. He visualized her thanking him for the office he had rendered her; the snatching of her from the clutches of a brutal husband.

He got up and paced the hut impatiently. He had been willing at last to let her go. But he was the one to take her down the river.

What right had any man to interfere? What right had she to accept such help from a stranger picked up in the backwoods of Canada?

He laughed hoarsely as he reflected that he who was strong and capable enough to run a logger crew was incapable of running his own wife. In every trick of the game she had beaten him, and she was beating him now in the last round. Shaggin was the trouble. He had given Shaggin his word to carry on. Confound Shaggin! What was Shaggin to him? He jammed on his hat and went across to Nicotte. She was sitting in her room sewing a new skin into her coat, when he entered.

'She – she come back?'

He shook his head and eyed her keenly.

'Nicotte, I'm going to be sick.'

'Eh!'

'I want you to give it round that I'm ill and – and my wife is looking after me – in the shack.'

'But I do not understand–'

'Logan will carry on for a day or two. If Shaggin returns tell him I'll be back in a few days – two, maybe.'

Nicotte's eyes narrowed as understanding slowly came. He was going after Conway, and did not want the affair bandied about the camp as it would be if the truth were suspected.

'Suppose Logan go to see you?'

'Tell him I don't want to see anyone. Light a fire over there to-morrow. It'll look better. And I want a pair of snow-shoes and a sleeping-bag.' He laughed grimly. 'Maybe I can dispense with the sleeping-bag. There won't be much time for that.'

'I find them,' she replied. 'When you go?'

'To-night – now.'

She went out and returned a few minutes later with the things he required. He took them silently and went to the door.

She hesitated a moment then: 'Douglas!' she cried, quickly.

He turned round and faced her.

'You – you won't keel him?'

He came towards her with wrinkled brow and seized her by the shoulders.

'Nicotte, you got hold of the wrong end of this. Susan had a strong reason for wanting to get to Vancouver. She took the first chance, and that's all there is to it.'

She stared up at him and remained silent. What was the use of telling him that for weeks Conway's eyes had been on Susan? What was the use of telling him that her woman's intuition saw more in this than a mere attempt at escape? He would never believe it.

Nicotte, who had had plenty of opportunity for studying men of Conway's type, had lost a lot of illusions. She ground her

169

white teeth and said nothing.

'It's all right, kid,' murmured Tearle. 'You just put that story around till I come back.'

She nodded and watched his big figure slip through the door. To her as to Susan he was a mystery. In a hundred ways he was so different from other men. At first she had really believed that he loved her as men love women; that Fate had flung her into a triangular drama from which she was powerless to free herself. But lately she had come to see. She saw him in a new light – a lonely man asking for something in vain, and in that knowledge her whole heart went out to him. Out of sympathy, perhaps, came the obsessive desire to be to him what Susan could not, or would not be.

All the quick passion of her was struggling for expression, and was only kept in check by the thought that it was ignoble; something less than the purer friendship he offered. It had pained and humiliated her to realize that the lamp which he had unwittingly lighted was doomed to burn unseen in her breast; that the wild love within her had to be controlled though it broke her heart. With the coming of this new development in Tearle's affairs was a chance to snatch a brand from the burning. A word – a mere suggestion – from her might have tipped the balance on her side. When he had gone she wondered why she had not done so. But in her wonderment came a whisper which was some alleviation to her aching heart. She had been true to her better self. For the first time in her life Nicotte had risen to great heights, and all because the man was different from other men who had admired her. Wherever his happiness lay she wanted him to get it. But she thought it did not lie out there on the trail with Susan.

Half an hour later Tearle emerged from the shack, with mittened hands and a pack on his back. He glanced up at the sky and was glad he had remembered the snow-shoes, for there were all the signs of an early fall. At the clump of firs by the lake he halted, and gazed across the open stretch of snow-encumbered land beyond. Somewhere out there was Susan – Susan who now probably deemed herself free of him for ever.

'Not yet,' he murmured. 'Not yet.' And with his head thrust forward in his aggressive way he plunged through the eerie gloom with his eyes fixed on the mule tracks which went winding away to the west.

CHAPTER FOURTEEN

Amazement was young Simpson's only emotion when Conway had stopped the mules and told him Susan was going to accompany them. In the ordinary way there would have been nothing remarkable in a woman accepting such an escort in Western Canada, but here a different set of circumstances came to complicate matters. This woman was leaving without the knowledge of her husband, and furthermore she was entrusting herself to a man whom Simpson knew to be as unscrupulous as he was cunning.

So astonished had he been at hearing the news, that he forgot to put the hundred and one questions which simmered in the back of his mind. Before he could recover, Susan had come running across the snow. Conway smiled at her and took some baggage from one of the mules that she might mount.

'I can walk,' she protested.

'Nonsense! There is not the slightest need. Please accept the best we can offer.'

Since he had already arranged a seat for her it seemed ungracious to refuse, and a few seconds later she was sitting across the improvised saddle gazing wistfully down the trail. With the first step of the animal came queer mental questioning. She turned her head and saw the shack disappearing behind the brown fir trunks. It was the last she would see of that, she thought, the last she would see of Tearle, too! She had not imagined she would experience any regret at leaving, and yet – and yet– It was strange how painful partings were, even though it was from a past that had offered small happiness. She instinctively disliked taking any new turning in life, no matter under what impelling power.

She imagined Tearle coming home, calling her and finding she was not in. He would not guess the truth for some time. The mere fact that he had permitted her to roam at large without questioning her, without exhibiting the slightest interest in what she had been doing or thinking, convinced her that for a long time he had not considered such a step as this on her part. She remembered the time she had taunted him, and he vowed he would bring her back again. But things had changed since then. Nicotte would have cancelled that intention.

It only needed the introduction of Nicotte into her thoughts to drive out any lingering regret. The insult he had placed upon her went very deep. Brutality, neglect, anything were better than cruel deception.

No, with Nicotte now free to enchant him with her roguish smiles and subtle fascination, Tearle would doubtless be content to accept the loss with even more than his usual equanimity. She blamed him not so much on account of the forbidden love as for the secrecy with which he had indulged in it. He had gone to Shaggin's quarters under the pretext of being near the men. All the time he had been putting forward work as an excuse for his isolation Nicotte had been– Ugh! she dared not reflect on it.

The trail which they were following left the river bank and turned abruptly inland to skirt a towering bluff whose sides went almost perpendicularly down to the water. The scene before her was one of entrancing beauty. Their way lay through a ravine down which a placid stream, now covered with thick ice, ran parallel with the fringe of the woods. On either side the trees clambered up the steep gradients, firs and silver beech all gorgeously arrayed in winter garments. The air was dry and clear and stung the face where it was exposed, sending the blood leaping madly through every vein.

It was a recrudescence of the past – of the days spent with Tearle when things were not so bad. There had been no dazzling snow then, no keen, life-giving ice-cold air, but the sensation was similar. She wanted to cry aloud with the joy of the wanderer, but something prevented that. Beautiful and entrancing as it was she felt alone.

At noon they stopped and boiled a kettle with the aid of a spirit lamp. Hot coffee followed and sandwiches made from canned meat and bread which she herself had made only yesterday. Simpson watched her with interrogative eyes, but he said nothing for he knew not what to say. When he did eventually open his mouth Conway sent him away to feed the mules. The boy scowled as he obeyed.

'I'll not be sorry to part company with that youth,' said Conway. 'I think he'd murder me if I gave him the chance.'

'But why?'

'Heaven knows. There are some people who without rhyme or reason take a violent dislike to others. Simpson is that way towards me.'

'You are like that towards him, too.'

'Perhaps.'

'You sent him away just now because he was about to speak to me. Why did you do that? Do you begrudge him a little conversation?'

Conway frowned and looked towards Simpson, who was turning out some fodder from a sack.

'Isn't it advisable not to have him poking his nose into this?' he murmured.

'Into what?'

175

'Into this – domestic tragedy.'

Susan's face went crimson. In the circumstances the words were a little brutal.

'There is no tragedy,' she retorted. 'I don't understand you.'

'Not in leaving your husband without notice?'

'No. He will understand. I shall wait for him at Vancouver.'

Conway's lips moved in an incredulous smile. She realized that in the face of what had happened it was useless to try to mislead him. But to air her troubles before another was ignominious, to say the least.

'You don't believe me?' she asked, indignant.

'Please don't put it that way,' he replied suavely. 'But I must confess that to me it is incredible that you will ever want to see him again – after what has happened.'

It silenced her effectually. But strangely enough she hated him to judge Tearle's conduct; resented what she felt his intrusion. Deep as Tearle's action rankled, she felt the desire – a foolish, quixotic desire perhaps – to defend him in his absence. Whatever he might be, Tearle had a thousand good points. He had brought her all across the wilderness safely. When she had been the means of losing the results of his arduous toil, Tearle had not uttered one word of reproach. She remembered, too, the nights

Tearle had watched over her in the vast, un-peopled spaces, and she had slept knowing that in his care she was as safe as in the little cottage at Lifton.

Strange that such thoughts should come to her now, when she was fleeing from him! Strange that she could think of him at all gently at that moment when he might be in another woman's arms.

'How did it all come about?' asked Con-way, rousing her from her reverie.

'What?'

'This – this unhappy marriage?'

Her eyes blazed with resentment at the intimate question, but before she could speak, Conway, seeing, went on.

'Very well,' he murmured, 'I'm sorry if you misinterpret sympathy as mere inquisitive-ness.'

His voice was so modulated as to convey the impression that she had hurt him deeply. Out of gratitude she was quickly repentant.

'Forgive me, but you must realize that such a discussion is painful to me. Whatever is done, is done. I can't bear to speak of it even to you who have helped me so much. Won't you forget it?'

'Certainly! Will you have some more coffee?'

They started away soon after, over the untrodden snow through a fairyland of dream-like colour schemes that bewildered

177

the eye with subtle changes as the configuration of the country altered. Occasionally, they saw in the distance quaint settlements lying chiefly along the line of the river, with here and there an isolated hut.

Nightfall found them again in thick timber. A magnificent sunset ushered in the great cold of evening, but the brilliant stars were soon obliterated by clouds and a keen wind which came out of the north.

'Feels like snow,' said Conway. 'Unfortunately we only have one tent. Simpson and I will use our sleeping-bags outside.'

She started to argue, but the two men would hear of nothing else. Despite everything she slept well and awoke to find it snowing gently. Any great fall would have arrested progress, but Conway was convinced that it would lift very soon, and after breakfast the journey was resumed.

During the day Simpson managed to get a few words in with Susan. He had ample time to reflect upon the situation, but he had got no nearer to a solution.

'Why did you come?' he asked.

The blunt question astonished Susan, but plain-spoken Simpson could put blunt questions without arousing resentment.

'Why shouldn't I come?' she wanted to know.

'I don't know, but I wish to God we were at Vancouver.'

'You say strange things. I am enjoying the trip immensely.'

'If I knew more perhaps I should enjoy it, Mrs Tearle,' he went on rapidly. 'There's something I don't understand – maybe you think I've no right to understand. But I'm afraid.'

She opened her eyes wide and laughed.

'Afraid? Of what?'

'Of Conway. Oh, I know you'll think I'm insane. You think I've got some sort of a grudge against him. I have: but not without good reason. Listen, there was a girl down–'

Susan put her hands to her ears.

'I won't listen to you,' she cried angrily.

'No,' he said bitingly, 'you'll listen to Conway, and that will be the end of everything. Now you're furious. So you ought to be. I know I've no right to interfere, but I simply can't sit still and think about possibilities–'

'What are you saying?'

'Tell me one thing and then I'll make it clear.'

'What do you want me to tell you?'

'What persuaded you to leave your husband so suddenly and shunt off with us? That's the mystery I want to solve.'

She controlled her rising anger and answered him coldly.

'It's no mystery to me. I have very sound reasons for all I do, and those reasons are entirely my own affair.'

'It's any fellow's affair who wants to prevent–'

He stumbled over the last word, and grew confused and incoherent. Only his face revealed the struggle taking place within him, his impulsive nature against his self-control. She pitied him, for at least his motive was good.

'There is no need to warn me – against anything,' she murmured. 'I know exactly what I am doing. It's good of you to have regard for my – my welfare, but it is impossible for you to understand.'

Conway's appearance put an end to further talk. Simpson moved away with the feeling that he had bungled everything in his impulsiveness. She imagined that he was merely intruding into her personal affairs. It was clear to him that she could see no farther than that. What exercised Simpson's mind was the suspicion that Conway was playing a deep game, and that with all her pride and self-possession Susan was going to fall into his net – that she had indeed already done so, though what means Conway had employed to get her so far he could not guess.

The snow continued until well into the afternoon, but it was not dense, and its total measure was less than four inches. With the clearing of the sky, the temperature in the shade fell sharply. The new snow glistened with a trillion points in the declining sun, and all the landscape to the west was robed in amber. It changed to pink and rose as the shadows lengthened and then faded into darker and more mysterious hues. When all the valley was darkened the mountain tops in the distance still held a noose of blood-red, which mounted and mounted until the peaks themselves were forced to give it up. The intensely cold night came down.

The camp was pitched as it was the evening before – under the side of a hill which served as a buttress to the prevailing wind. Simpson lopped branches from the neighbouring trees, and soon a fire was going, and supper prepared.

'Two days gone,' mused Conway. 'Time flies all too quickly. You'll need to tuck yourself up well to-night, for it's well below zero.'

'You and Mr Simpson take the tent to-night,' she pleaded. 'Let me share the discomforts.'

'And sleep out?'

Both men smiled amusedly.

'I'm much harder than you imagine,' she argued, with a smile.

But she did not look hard as she sat there in the ruddy glow of the fire. She had removed her hat and her heavy coat and looked the embodiment of all that was feminine. The open-air life was already working miracles with her. In the lumber camp she had grown a little pallid and listless, for always her soul had revolted against the smells and heat of that airless cook-house. Now her eyes were bright again, and her cheeks filling out to deepen the dimples on either side.

The admiration in Conway's eyes as he watched her was unmistakable. His hand trembled as he raised his cup to his lips and within him surged passions difficult to control. The by-play did not escape the observant and silent Simpson, watching him out of the corner of his eye.

It was an hour later when Susan retired after shaking hands with them both. The day had been long and she felt healthily tired and ready for the blessed oblivion of sleep. In four days, all being well, she would be in Vancouver. What she intended doing when she arrived was not yet clear, but in the back of her mind was Uncle Peter. Surely Uncle Peter would cable a sum sufficient to get her home.

That thought should have been a balm to her, but it was not. Home might be beautiful, but it would be different now. Gone for ever were those careless days. A man had made all that seem like wasted time. That was her last thought before sleep came and dulled her mind. A man had taken her heart from her bosom and trampled on it!

Conway and Simpson sat by the fire for some time, both plunged in silence, the man smoking and the boy gazing into the burning brands. At last Conway stretched himself and picked up his sleeping-bag.

'I'm turning in,' he yawned. 'Better get some more firewood before you do likewise.'

Simpson nodded, and taking the small axe and lantern wandered across to some young trees on which the branches grew low down. He hacked away for some time, and having cut sufficient to keep the fire going until morning, went back to the camp.

About twenty yards away, he stopped dead. Creeping towards the tent was the tall figure of Conway clearly silhouetted in the glow of the fire. Simpson saw him reach the tent and listen intently. He saw him fumbling with the strings. The youth dropped his load and leapt forward with the agility of a cat, the axe raised in his hand.

'Conway!'

Conway started and turned swiftly.

'What are you doing there?'

The words spat furiously from the boy's mouth. Conway stared at him for a second and then shrugged his shoulders and walked back to the fire. Simpson leapt and caught him by the arm.

'You skunk!' he snarled.

'Eh!'

'Listen,' he said hoarsely. 'We're going to take her safely to Vancouver and all the way we're going to act on the level. If that happens again I'll deal with you.'

'You poor fool!' snapped Conway. 'Do you imagine–'

His threatening approach was stopped by a threatening movement of the axe. In the shining eyes behind it he saw written such dogged and fearless determination as he had never believed his contemptible assistant capable of.

'I think you have gone mad,' he said, sneering, and taking his sleeping-bag moved to the trunk of a giant fir which overhung the camp. Simpson went back for his fuel, and made up the fire. Then he stretched himself between it and the tent.

CHAPTER FIFTEEN

All through the night Tearle followed the winding trail, moving along mechanically wherever the deep impressions of the mules' feet led him. By this means he reckoned to reduce Conway's lead by at least eight hours and to overtake him by the evening of the following day.

At dawn he rested for an hour, and ate some food, which he sorely needed. Coming on top of the long walk of the day before the nocturnal march was a herculean task and his limbs felt heavy as lead. But he was not the man to yield to physical suffering when big things were at stake, and immediately he had finished his scanty meal he was off again.

His programme was destined to be changed, for a few minutes after starting, light powdery snow commenced to fall from the overcast sky. He swore loudly and quickened his gait to make the most of the time left to him before the tracks should be snowed over. For two hours the going was comparatively easy, and then the tracks gradually disappeared. He was left in an unmarked wilderness. Two miles away, dimly seen through the grey curtain of falling snow, was a thick wood. He made for that and was fortunate in picking up the tracks again, for the trees had served as a partial shield to the obliterating blanket.

On leaving the timber he was faced again by the old problem. That Conway had taken the Vancouver route was beyond question, but which was the Vancouver route he did not know. In this maze of hills and ravines to find three people was like looking for a needle in a haystack. He broke across the open space and plunged onward until he struck the timber again. But he wandered on the fringe of the wood for two hours before he was successful in his search.

Following the faint tracks like a sleuth-hound he emerged in a long narrow ravine. It was now past noon, and his strength, great as it was, was rapidly diminishing. He could do no more than drag one leg after the other with an effort that was painful to his brain. But the snow had lifted and the tracks were discernible. Knowing that thereafter they could be easily followed he succumbed to the demands of his physical being, and flinging off the heavy pack dropped down and went to sleep.

When he awoke he was irritated to find it was night – and not only night but near to daybreak. Twelve hours wasted! He up-braided himself severely, forgetting that since he last had slept he had covered more than fifty miles of forbidding country. His limbs were almost frozen and icicles hung from the fringe of his cap where his breath had condensed. He jumped about, banging his hands on his legs and thighs until the circulation came back and his blood ran like red-hot needles within his veins.

He felt better after that, but mightily hungry from the great loss of body heat. He lighted the spirit stove which he carried and melted down some snow in order to make tea. Twenty minutes later he felt like a new being and was ready for anything. Over the snow he went again at a mile-eating pace, falling occasionally into drifts and losing the tracks for short distances. By noon he reckoned he had gained miles. He ate rapidly and set his nose to the trail again.

An hour later he was rewarded by catching a glimpse of his quarry. The trail led over a mountain in zigzag fashion, rising and rising until he thought it would never end. But at last he came to the summit and was afforded a magnificent view of all the land to the west. Away in the blue distance his keen eyes observed a collection of black dots – two animals and some figures. For a few seconds they remained in view and then were lost in the undulations.

'Got 'em!' he ejaculated.

But he reckoned without the elements.

Away in the north great forces were gathering. Tearle's first warning of them was an icy blast which lifted the loose snow from the tops of the mountains and flung it willy-nilly down the precipitous slopes. In the blue distance changes were taking place. The sunlight disappeared and the horizon grew hazy and grey. Soon the ragged edge of the creeping cloud obtruded across the blue, increasing in speed as he looked. Another gust of freezing wind smote through the clothes he wore and brought him to realize that things were going to be bad.

Gone was all the sunshine. The whole landscape was plunged in gloom and on the wind came particles of snow driven almost horizontally. He pulled down the flaps of his cap and plunged forward at reckless pace, knowing that in a short time nothing would be left of the guiding tracks.

Half an hour passed before the blizzard really broke loose. The intermittent gusts amalgamated into one appalling 'pushing' wind. It howled and shrieked like ten thousand demons. It lifted the snow in huge white masses, driving it into mouth, eyes, and face, almost tearing the flesh from the exposed parts. Which came from the earth and which from the sky it was impossible to tell. At times the force of the wind held him stationary; at others it sent him tottering on hands and knees.

He was at the very worst part of his journey, on a narrow ledge overlooking a ravine, the bottom of which was a whirling mass of snow. The mouth of the ravine faced the direction of the wind and acted as a free tunnel for all its force. Shelter there was none, for the rock on his right side went up sheer. He thought of the party ahead and hoped for Susan's sake they were out of his death-trap.

Crash! A great mass of granite, loosened by the wind from some height above, hit the ledge not twenty yards from him and went smashing down into the ravine. For nearly a minute its mighty reverberations echoed like thunder all down the valley. It had taken with it tons of rock from the ledge and left barely sufficient space for him to creep by.

As white as the snow itself he continued to make progress, fighting for breath and clutching at any useful projections on the rock wall. The snow on the ledge lay a foot deep and formed a treacherous foothold. When things were at their worst and he was compelled to crouch under the wall and shield his face from the cruel wind there came a temporary lull, although the snow fell even more thickly. He rose swiftly and determined to make the most of this respite. But he had not gone more than twenty yards when his glance fell on the strings of a fur cap protruding from the snow. He stooped and pulled at it. The cap itself came to view, frozen stiff.

The significance of this find was not lost on him. That it belonged to one of the two men was certain — but which? And what could have happened to cause one of them to leave so precious a thing behind? He glanced over the rock and saw distinctly the impress of limbs or a body, on a sloping projection four feet down.

Craning his neck forward, his vision managed to penetrate the falling snow to the bottom of the ravine. He uttered a groan as a blob of black came to view — a still body! Then came a dreadful thought— Susan! It was true Susan had no cap like this, but that did not signify that the cap belonged to the body. There might be more than one down there! The whole party might easily have been swept from this perilous ledge!

He ran along the ledge seeking a way down, but it was some time before he found a possible means of descent, and that was so precipitous that anything less than a mountain goat might have recoiled from it. But he did not hesitate. He knew he must risk it.

His descent was a series of great slides, each one ending in a painful bump against some half-hidden rock. When at last he reached the bottom his body was bruised and torn in a hundred different places. He peered through the falling snow and saw the black blob away to his left. Apprehensive, he plunged forward and fell on his knees beside it. The face was completely snowed up and he feared that he had come too late. He brushed the light covering away with his hand until the blue flesh came to view.

'Simpson!'

He dragged the body across his knee and inclined his head towards the chest, but he was unable to distinguish any heartbeat. There was no time to look around for any further victims, for Simpson was either dead or as near as it was possible to be. Hastily he loosened his pack and searched for the small flask of brandy he had brought with him. He found it and forced the end of the flask between the blue lips. For a time nothing happened. He waited for a few minutes and tried again. An eyelid quivered and the slightest of sounds came from between the lips.

Then the life-giving spirit began to have effect. While he was rubbing the limbs vigorously Simpson opened his eyes. They rested on Tearle for a full minute before their owner could sort out his senses.

'Tearle!' he whispered weakly between half-frozen lips.

Tearle stopped him.

'Don't try talking, sonny; it'll sure hurt,' he advised.

Simpson's wondering eyes were roaming over his rescuer. He was apparently finding it difficult to piece the disintegrated past into intelligible sequence.

'What – what's happened, Tearle?' he whispered.

'You got blown over the cliff by a blizzard. That's better. You're beginning to look less like a dead man. Hello – what's this?'

'This' was a frozen clot of blood on the hair behind Simpson's ear. Tearle pulled it aside and saw a nasty wound beneath. Then he ran his fingers deftly over the body.

'Any bones broken?'

'My arm,' groaned Simpson.

Tearle lifted the left arm gently and found it broken just below the elbow.

'Got to see to that at once,' he ejaculated. He left Simpson the brandy flask and hunted round for two suitable sticks to serve as splints. With them and two handkerchiefs he bound the broken arm.

'How are you feeling?' he queried.

'Not so bad.'

'Can you walk?'

'I'll try.'

'Good. There's a kind of cave along there. It'll be warmer inside than out.'

With the help of his supporting arm the dazed and suffering boy managed to reach the cavern in the rock. He sank down weakly, and Tearle, realizing that he was in need of food, commenced to prepare some.

Simpson's eyes followed him closely. A queer look came over him as he reconstructed the immediate past. He was waiting for Tearle to bombard him with questions, but Tearle seemed to be immersed in his task. To Simpson this was extraordinary, the man was not human. Surely his first thought should be of his wife's welfare. He failed fully to appreciate Tearle's methodical temperament; the desire to meet troubles in strict rotation. At this moment Simpson came first in Tearle's opinion. Susan could wait awhile.

'I suppose the others got through safely?' he queried, without looking round.

'Yes, yes.'

'It's queer that Conway didn't come and look for you.'

The growl of insensate rage from Simpson's lips brought his head round slowly.

'Feeling bad again?' he asked.

'Yes – I feel– Tearle, you don't understand what's happened. You're thinking I fell over the ledge?'

'Naturally.'

'Well, I didn't.'

Tearle, believing the boy's mind must be wandering, spoke soothingly to him as to a child.

'How then did you get where I found you?'

The boy's mouth twitched and his hands

closed and unclosed.

Tearle watched him keenly as he attended to the boiling of the kettle.

'I didn't fall over,' burst out Simpson in rage. 'I was pushed over by that dirty skunk!'

'Eh!'

'It's true. He had been waiting for a chance to get rid of me. The blizzard came down and gave it to him. We were all huddled up together. Susan was on the inside and didn't see what happened. Conway waited until I was near the edge and then he kicked the mule from his side. The beast shoved its haunches round and got me fair and square. I don't remember any more.'

Tearle's crouching figure was still as a piece of rock. When he spoke it was in a hoarse whisper.

'Why did he want to get rid of you? Why?'

'You – you don't know?'

Tearle knew. There had been no need to put the question at all. Simpson saw a quiver in the muscles of his face and heard the quick intake of his breath. But his silence was more ominous than volumes of threats and imprecations.

'Didn't you know – before?'

Tearle shook his head.

'I guess I'm a bit of a blind fool where creatures like Conway are concerned.

Maybe we'll have something to say to each other – when we meet.'

'Susan doesn't know, Tearle. She trusted him. She thought he was straight. I tried to tell her, but she imagined I had a grudge against him. Tearle, you'd better go now. Leave me here with a bit of food. I'll do for a bit–'

Tearle shook his head stubbornly.

'One thing at a time. I'll get him all right – later.'

'But you must think of the danger–'

'What danger?'

'Great God!' cried the boy, almost hysterically. 'Can't you grasp realities? Why do you think he wanted to get me out of the way? I tell you he's all that's crooked. To-night they'll be alone. To-night anything may happen–'

Tearle stared at the blank wall opposite. Strange as it might seem what Simpson hinted at had never crossed his mind. He was so much the idealist, it needed a violent pull on his imagination to force him to see the truth. Simpson's excited and horrified eyes were achieving this end.

'Kid, do you know what you're saying?' he begged, his brain afire.

Simpson nodded slowly.

'Yes, I know,' he said slowly. 'Only too well. And that's why I tell you not to wait a second but to go now, before it's too late.'

'I'll go,' growled Tearle, and, his lips set in the same grim line he had set them on another memorable occasion long past, he went on: 'but I'll take you with me. Here, drink this!'

CHAPTER SIXTEEN

The full force of the blizzard had caught Susan's party on the perilous ledge above the ravine. New to such an experience, it had filled her with terror. Under normal conditions the path was dizzy enough, but with that wild wind shrieking in her face it took all her courage to prevent her from giving way to hysteria. At its start, Conway brought the leading mule abreast of her that she might benefit from such protection as its body offered. When the dreadful catastrophe took place her mind was too confused to realize it. All she heard was a low gasp, almost like a cough, and a dull thud. Some seconds passed before she became aware that Simpson was no longer there. She turned her head and looked back through the whirling snow, but the second mule was without its attendant.

'Simpson!' she gasped.

Conway pointed down the ravine, his lips moving nervously.

'Has he fallen?'

'Slipped,' he yelled. 'Stead-dee!' This to the mule.

A wail of horror broke from her.

'Courage! We'll get through,' shouted Conway.

'But Simpson! We must go to him! Oh, we must! He may be mortally injured down there.'

He caught her trembling, heavily gloved hand and put his lips close to her ear.

'No use,' he yelled. 'He's lost. There's a two-hundred-foot drop from top to bottom. We can do nothing.'

'We must!'

'Look for yourself. You'll see how impossible it is.'

But she shook her head. The chasm had claimed one victim, and it was more frightful than ever to her.

'Poor devil!' muttered Conway, and jerked the leader mule forward.

They proceeded at a snail's pace, blinded by the driving snow and buffeted by the raging wind. Susan, jammed against the wall by the mule's body, felt sick and ill. She could not help feeling that something ought to have been done about Simpson, but exactly what was not easy to determine. After half an hour of physical torture and mental agony the wind lifted slightly. The pass merged into a broader track, which left the side of the ravine and went down between towering rocks to the lower altitudes.

Susan again mounted the mule, and for

over an hour rode along in silence. The fate of poor Simpson affected her deeply. There was much in the boy's passionate and impulsive nature which had appealed to her; moreover, she had regarded him as a kind of chaperon. Now that he was gone, strange apprehensions possessed her, in spite of all her striving to banish them since there seemed to be no grounds for them, but as the darkness began to fall they came swarming over her once more.

'The storm seems to have passed,' said Conway, in a much relieved tone of voice. 'We must camp as soon as we reach timber.'

The instinct of woman, it must have been, whose dimly heard warning took away any joy at the prospect of a rest. A little farther on they were obliged to halt that Conway might put on his snow-shoes, for the snow in the valley was deep and soft. By the time they started again the light had all but gone. On the skyline, dimly visible, was the black bulk of the woods. Conway turned the mules' heads in that direction.

The sky cleared before they reached their objective, and the welcome stars blazed down to light their way. The land rose again in a great sweep and the mules struggled up it to the fringe of the wood. There Conway halted them and assisted Susan to dismount. The place seemed particularly desolate, and the undefinable fears which had been haunting her grew apace. She felt she wanted to be near other people – any kind of people.

'I'll gather some wood,' said Conway. 'Will you get some of the packs off?'

She nodded mechanically and went to the two mules which Conway had driven under the trees. The few extra feet of elevation afforded her a view of the river below, a silver band in the brooding darkness. A low exclamation left her lips as she saw scattered lights gleaming between the branches of a tree below her. She changed her position so that the tree was no longer an obstacle, and her heart leaped with joy to behold what was undoubtedly a township on the near bank of the river.

'Mr Conway!' she cried.

'Hello!'

'Please come here!'

He joined her a minute later and followed the line of her pointing finger.

'Look! A town! There is no need to camp here to-night. It can't be more than a mile distant.'

She strove to hide her eagerness to go on, but Conway knew it well enough.

'That must be Roaring Forks,' he nodded. 'It would be far wiser to camp here, though. There is only one hotel there, the resort of men engaged in the wood-pulp business. It's the roughest place in Western Canada.'

'Let us try it, anyway,' she pleaded. 'I want to sleep under a roof to-night. I'm cold and–'

'I'll soon have a fire going–'

'No. To-night I'm distraught. I can't help thinking of that poor boy. Besides, you must do something about him. You must get help and find his body.'

'What good would that do?'

'Mr Conway!' she exclaimed, inexpressibly shocked at his callousness. 'Oh, how can you! I can't bear to think of him lying out there in the cold! It's horrible. He was our comrade; so young, too! What are you going to say to his people? That you left him dead in the snow? Can't you see how heartless such a thing would be? You must go out and bring him back.'

But it was not entirely on Simpson's behalf that she made this plea, deeply affected as she was in this respect. Roaring Forks, unruly and rough as it might prove, was preferable to the great silence of the woods.

'In all probability there will be no accommodation in Roaring Forks,' argued Conway.

'Let us try.'

Reluctantly he agreed. Leading the two mules they went down the slope to the river bank, and in less than half an hour were entering the town. It presented a strange and beautiful sight to her. Over the new snow the lights from the windows of the scattered dwelling-houses were weaving fantastic designs in black and white and amber. Away to the right she caught a glimpse of a factory of huge dimensions – a squat mass frowning upon the relatively tiny shacks.

In the centre of the main thoroughfare was a blaze of light, and reaching from end to end of the tall wooden building from which this came, was a board bearing the words, 'Roaring Forks Hotel.' As they approached it a babble of noises broke on the still, keen air, mingled with a wheezy note of a violin and the thump of a piano.

She was not long before she realized that Conway had not exaggerated when he averred that Roaring Forks was rough. The inside of the hotel was an inferno. Dancing and gambling were in full swing and the atmosphere was choked with tobacco smoke and dust. A few women were in evidence, but they were strange and mysterious creatures who stared curiously at her as she entered.

She sat on a bench slightly removed from the vociferous crowd while Conway hunted up the proprietor, who was indulging in a furious game of faro at one of the tables. At length he was cajoled into attending to his legitimate business, and with his hands thrust deep in his pockets came to have a look at Susan, probably to satisfy himself that she was not in league with her companion to report him for a flagrant violation of the prohibition law.

'Married?' he queried to Susan's horror.

Conway laughed easily and shook his head.

'We want two rooms. Can you manage it?'

As she waited for his return, Susan could not help wondering whether this was much of an improvement upon camping. In the blaze of light and the din of human voices it was easy to reproach herself for her recent nervousness. What had caused it? Why, after all these months of wandering and self-sufficiency, had she permitted herself to be afraid?

The landlord lurched back and hic-coughed that he could accommodate them. While a shock-headed boy showed Susan up to her room Conway went out to stable the mules. Susan found her room a box-like affair on the top floor. Nevertheless it was fairly clean and cosy, boasting electric light, which was presumably generated by the Company which ran the factory.

After a wash and general clean-up she felt more cheerful. But a gnawing hunger possessed her, and she wondered where one ate in such a place. She rang the bell and after a long wait the shock-haired lad knocked and came in.

'I want some food,' she announced. 'Where can I get it?'

'The guy you came with ordered supper to be brought up to his room.'

'But I don't want mine in his room. I want it here.'

He scratched his head and muttered something about being too busy to go running around for people who changed their minds. Then he disappeared. She waited a considerable time, but he showed no sign of returning. She was about to ring the bell again when a knock sounded on the door.

'Come in!' she cried.

To her astonishment Conway entered.

'Aren't you coming to have something to eat?' he queried.

'I'm waiting for it.'

'But I ordered it to be sent to my room. It's there now.'

'Why did you do that?' she asked quickly, annoyed.

'What else could I do? There is no place downstairs. In the evening the dining-room is given up to dancing. I'm sorry if I have offended you. Shall I bring yours up here?'

'Yes, please.'

He was about to leave when she changed her mind and put aside her doubts.

'Never mind. I'll go with you,' she said steadily.

'Good. You must be hungry. I am famished.'

Conway's room was fairly commodious, a kind of bed-sitting-room with a dividing curtain across the centre. The curtain was drawn when Susan entered with the surveyor, and an appetizing meal was spread on a small table near the window. The man waited until she was seated and then took the chair opposite and proceeded to open a bottle of champagne. He poured some into each of the glasses, but Susan shook her head.

'Do,' he pleaded. 'Eat, drink and be merry; and forget the past.'

She shuddered at the words. Forget the past! It seemed cruel to utter such a sentiment.

'When are you going back for Simpson?' she asked in a tremulous voice.

'To-morrow. Nothing can be done to-night. I promise you to start off early in the morning with a dog-team. I have already arranged it with the landlord.'

He raised his glass and toasted the future, but she did not join him. Now that they were half-way to their destination the future seemed even less rosy than before. The first excitement of escape had worn off. She could not help thinking of Tearle back there in the lumber camp. By this time would he have become reconciled to the change? Yes, she told herself. Tearle was not the type of man to be knocked down by a thing like this, even if he cared for her. She laughed bitterly as she reflected upon the extent of his devotion. Conway, finishing another glass of champagne, looked at her keenly.

'Why the merriment?'

'Did it sound like merriment?' she asked.

'No, I'm damned if it did. Susan, can't you forget him?'

The amazing remark caused her to start and bite her lips. Under the influence of the drink Conway was changing, swiftly reaching a stage of hilarity and nonchalance. By an obvious effort he strove to affect a deeply serious and sympathetic mood.

'You were thinking of him, weren't you?' he murmured.

'Suppose I was?'

'It's foolish. Does he merit any further consideration from you? All along he has deceived you. He never has cared for you as a man should care for his wife. I knew it back there where I first met you. It only needed that girl Nicotte to arouse something in him you never succeeded in arousing.'

'Don't – don't!' she moaned, then she changed to indignation. 'I asked you to take me to Vancouver, not to become a judge of my husband!'

'It's for any man to judge another who acts as a blackguard.'

'I won't listen to you!' she flamed. 'Whatever he may be it is for me alone to accuse him. What is it to you?'

Her indignant query gave him a lead to the thing he wanted to say. She saw his eyes blaze with passion. Suddenly he put his hand across the table and grasped hers tightly.

'What is it to me?' he repeated tensely. 'And you can ask that! You who must know it's everything in the world! You do know it, don't you?'

'I don't understand you.' Susan's hardly uttered reply was cold.

'Then it's time you did,' he went on, bluntly sharp. 'Susan, I love you with every atom of my strength. I love you as I've never loved anything in this world. I loved you the moment I saw you. I–'

With a gasp of horror she snatched her hand away and sprang to her feet.

'How dare you say that?' Her voice was tense, hard, though her brain was aflame.

Conway laughed exultingly.

'Dare! There's nothing I wouldn't dare – for you. Why shouldn't I tell you this? You are free to love again–'

In a twinkling he was a different man from the suave, attentive one who had been her travelling companion. Words which had been bubbling on his lips for weeks past broke all barriers. Restraint and discretion were flung to the winds. He had meant to tell her this in the silent confines of the woods. By some strange divination the woman's inner self had known it and had recoiled before it. She saw him now leaning over her in an almost threatening attitude, and the repulsive light in his eyes was eloquent of the forces that swayed him.

'It is unspeakable you should talk like this to me!' she flared. 'This is the end of our friendship – the end.'

In two bounds she was at the door, but found her arm caught firmly in his hand. Her struggles to free herself only brought her closer to him, so close that she was conscious of a nausea.

'Friendship?' he taunted. 'Did you imagine it was only friendship I desired? That may have been good enough for a husband – but not for a lover.'

At last anger overcame her fear. She brought her hand up and hit him as hard as she could on the side of the face.

'You brute!'

'You – you–' he grunted. 'You shall pay for that!'

He leaped past her, and turning the key in the lock put it in his pocket.

'Put that back!' she demanded.

'Not yet,' was the cool response.

While she unavailingly struggled with the strong door he went to the table, poured out what remained of the champagne, and gulped it down in one draught.

'I wanted to be reasonable,' he said thickly, as he turned to her.

'Let – let me go! I ought never to have entered this place!'

His only response was to advance towards her with open arms. She eluded him and opened her mouth to cry for help.

'That won't help you,' he sneered. 'They wouldn't hear a gunshot downstairs. You got yourself into this fix. You yourself have just cancelled our friendship. What remains after that, eh?'

Driven to frenzy she snatched a knife from the table and extended its point towards him.

'Don't come near me,' she cried hysterically. 'If you touch me I'll – I'll–'

An incredulous laugh. But what Conway took for dramatics was dead seriousness with Susan Tearle. He underrated her determination. In his colossal misunderstanding of her nature he believed her merely acting. Flinging the table aside he drove her before him until her back came up against the wall, sharply.

'If you – if you–' Once more she gave him warning – warning, had the man really known her, he would have heeded.

But he still came on, half drunk and triumphant. His arm reached out and caught her round the neck. The next instant the knife came down swiftly. A queer cough issued from his throat. He spun half round and fell with a thud on the floor. The knife dropped from the woman's fingers and she stood dumb, the shriek of horror that had started frozen on her palsied lips.

Then there was no sound. Nothing but the drone of voices and music from far below. Conway lay where he had fallen, a pool of crimson slowly forming on the carpet. A terror, surpassing anything she had ever known, possessed Susan Tearle. For minutes she was incapable of thought. When the reeling brain began to function again it pulsated with but one great desire – to get away from the man she had stabbed.

She staggered across to the door, forgetting that the key was in Conway's pocket. Twice she tried to approach that still form, to be brought to a halt within two paces of it… At last she summoned all her courage, and with eyes averted felt in his side pocket.

With the key she turned to the door. The lock was turned. The opening door brought a gust of fresh air along the corridor. She tottered out and had reached the top of the staircase when the sound of heavy steps coming towards her met her ears.

CHAPTER SEVENTEEN

She wanted to run, to hide her guilty face from whoever was coming, but she lacked the power to move. It was as if her will functioned in jerks, and having applied the brake she had lost the power with which to set free her body from the paralysis which gripped it.

A face came out of the darkness of the stairs, the last face on earth she expected to see. Tearle's. She swayed as she recognized her husband, and would have fallen but for his swift leap and the helping arm he extended.

'Douglas! Douglas!' she moaned, and her whole body shook in one racking shudder.

'What is it?' he begged. 'You screamed. I heard you!'

But instead, she demanded:

'What are you doing here?'

'That's the question I ought to ask you,' grimly he replied. 'Get your coat. We're leaving right now.'

She turned slowly and stared towards the open door at the end of the corridor. Again she shuddered, and her hands groped towards her husband. Tearle gazed at her with wrinkled brow. Her attitude! It was distinctly different from what he had expected.

'Is that your room?' he queried, seeing her stare.

'N-no,' she stammered, as her head shook.

'Then whose is it?' came the harsh demand. 'And why did you scream?'

'Douglas,' she burst out brokenly, 'oh, Douglas! Douglas! I've killed him – in there – in there–!'

His big hand gripped the balustrade and a groan came from his throat.

'So that's it,' he choked. 'You – you were in his room – and you've killed him!'

His mouth twitched in his agony of mind as he groped towards the open door. As in a dream Susan followed him. But she got no farther than the door. Nothing in the world would persuade her to enter that place again.

'Susan!'

She started at the exclamation and the voice, and swung around to behold Simpson with his arm in a sling and his head bandaged.

'How – how–?' She fairly gasped in her bewilderment, so much in keeping was this new and unexpected appearance, the reason for which she could not grasp with a brain that from whirling was becoming numbed, dull.

'I'm all right,' he replied swiftly. 'Where's

Tearle? And why do you look so ill?'

She pointed to the open door and Simpson glanced inside. A note of horror broke from his lips. With one swift glance at her he disappeared into the room. After a few minutes that seemed hours to the waiting woman, Simpson dashed out and ran down the stairs. Her horrified eyes followed him until he disappeared, and then switched back to the doorway to focus themselves on Tearle's grim face.

'Get your coat and other things,' he said. 'We're leaving this place.'

'I – I–'

'Get them!'

Automatically she moved at the word of command. It left her no freedom of action and in her heart she was glad, for her own brain was too disordered to function. She went to her room and gathered her few belongings together. Strangely the first great horror had gone. She was resigned to the situation. It was in self-defence, she argued. No woman could have acted differently. Her judge would understand. Surely they would understand!

Downstairs she found Tearle and Simpson waiting for her in the corridor, but the door of the room in which the dreadful thing had taken place was shut. She stopped a few feet from Tearle and looked at him.

'Ready?' he asked hoarsely.

She nodded in stony silence. Then suddenly her dazed brain grew clear and she realized what must be done.

'I – I can't go away,' she moaned. 'I did it! I'll tell them I did it. He was a brute and–'

Tearle caught her firmly by the arm.

'It's all right,' he muttered. 'There's a doctor looking after him now.'

'A doctor? You mean – I – I – didn't–'

'He'll be well in a week or two. Come! We're going!'

Unspeakable relief sent a gust of tears streaming from her eyes.

'Thank God!' she sobbed. 'Oh, thank God!'

So engrossed was she in her own affairs that without one question to Simpson about his miraculous escape she dully nodded him a good-bye, and followed Tearle downstairs and out of the place. He led the way along the river and up the steep ascent to a spot not far from the place which she and Conway had chosen for their camp a few hours before. While Tearle built a fire, no word was spoken. The sudden change in the situation bewildered her. When the fire was going merrily he came and put the sleeping-bag at her feet.

'What – what about you?' she quavered.

'I can manage,' he replied abruptly.

'Douglas!'

'Hello!'

'What are you going to do – about me?'

'We're going back to the lumber camp to-morrow.'

'No – no!'

He turned his head and stared at her hard.

'That can't be,' she choked. 'Let me go my own way to-morrow. Give me enough food to get me to Vancouver. I'll get there – somehow. That's all I ask of you. Surely you can't refuse me.'

'Why not?' he asked simply.

'Don't ask me to go into details – please! But isn't it clear to you that between us everything is ended?'

'Only one thing is clear to me,' he growled. 'And that is the sooner we get back to camp the better.'

She clenched her fists tightly.

'You mean you will take me back by force?'

'If necessary. I hope it won't be made necessary.'

A great sob left her lips at the thought of the ignominy he was placing upon her. To go back as his wife, with Nicotte–

'No, no! I won't come!' she cried. 'I won't!'

'I think,' said Douglas Tearle, 'you will. Better sleep now, it's late.'

'Douglas,' she pleaded. 'You are taking a step you will regret. I never dreamed you were capable of deliberately hurting a woman. Are you a brute, too?'

'Maybe!' he replied coldly.

Tearle sat over the fire long after she had snuggled down inside the sleeping-bag. The incident at Roaring Forks was like a red-hot needle in his brain. Although he was successful in reconstructing the scene there fairly accurately, it stung and tortured him. That Conway had got his deserts was but a small enough compensation for the blow to his pride. It savoured of some miserable and sordid affair of the slums. He could bear her apparent lovelessness for him, her fierce antagonism, but this. Faugh! It polluted the atmosphere.

It was clear enough to him that the bottom had been knocked out of this queerly sorted marriage. All that remained was the closing scene, which he vowed should take place as soon as he had fulfilled his promise to Shaggin. The moment Shaggin returned he meant to give her the freedom she pined for.

Huddled up close to the fire he tried to sleep, but failed to do more than doze intermittently. Long before sunrise he was preparing breakfast. When Susan awoke she found a meal waiting. With his usual, almost annoying, consideration he had refrained from starting to eat until she was ready to join him. Silently she drank the hot tea and ate the fried bacon.

'Have you changed your mind?' she inquired suddenly in a low voice. It was her first word of the day.

'There's no reason why I should. I guess you're my wife until I cut the bonds.'

'When are you going to do that?'

'When I'm through with Shaggin.'

'Your devotion to duty is extraordinary.'

'So is yours,' he retorted.

She saw a quarrel brewing, but at the last moment refrained from forcing it. One thing was certain. He was determined to take her back. Repellent as this course was to her, there was nothing to be gained by resistance. She helped him strike camp and insisted upon carrying some of the gear. A few minutes later they headed for the mountain path, the one where but yesterday Simpson had all but met his death. When they reached the spot she shuddered as she gazed over the edge of the ravine beneath, now clearly visible in the morning sunshine.

'Did you find Simpson – down there?' she asked.

'Yep.'

'And you managed to climb down?'

He nodded and shot her a swift glance as he heard the exclamation of admiring surprise from her lips.

'That – that man said it was impossible to get down. I wanted him to go–'

'He had his own reasons,' muttered Tearle, but added no explanation in the campaign of no explanations he had begun. But she did not miss the significance of his words. The thing they implied was horrible.

'I – I begged him to go,' she pleaded. 'When Simpson slipped–'

'Simpson didn't slip!'

'Didn't slip?'

'He was pushed over.'

Susan's knees gave way under her and she stood shakily as she stared at the maker of the astounding accusation in speechless amazement.

'Did Simpson say that?' she gasped.

'Yes.'

But so outrageously cruel was the thing that had happened the woman refrained from further questions. She could only try to think. It took her breath away. Who but a devil incarnate would have woven such a plot? And that was the man she had trusted! The knowledge of his perfidy and treachery helped to vindicate her recent action to her own conscience. The wounding seemed less savage now.

'The brute!' she said through her tightly clenched teeth.

'Just discovered that?' murmured Tearle.

'If you knew before why didn't you tell me? Why didn't you warn me against a man like that?'

'You were free to choose your own friends.'

'And you yours?' she retorted.

'That's so!'

How she believed she hated him for his terse rejoinders! If only he would do something – beat her, harangue her! She wanted some outlet for her pent-up emotions; some excuse to hurl at him the accusations that rankled in her bosom.

The day passed and another was born, a magnificent day that would have brought joy to any but dead hearts. Yet it was lived in almost complete silence. When the evening meal was over Tearle sat by the fire gazing reflectively into it and smoking pipe after pipe. Susan, less self-controlled, was on the verge of complete breakdown. Anything were better than this brooding atmosphere of bitter war.

'Douglas!' she at last broke silence plaintively.

He took the pipe from his lips and turned his head.

'Talk to me! For God's sake talk to me or I shall go mad.'

The wild look in her eyes held his gaze. The heaving bosom evidenced the depths of her emotion.

'I guess you're played out,' he murmured. 'Maybe it would have been better for us to have parted back there, but it was no fit place to leave a woman.'

'I know. You did right to bring me back, but can't we be friends until such time as we?– Douglas, I'm not blaming you for what you

219

did, in the circumstances, but you should have told me. It was the sudden discovery that – that drove me to desperation.'

His eyes narrowed at these words, for even now he had not the remotest idea of what she meant.

'You've got me guessing,' he muttered. 'What was it I did which drove you to desperation?'

'You mean you don't know?'

He shook his head slowly.

'I can't – I can't understand you. I've seen it with my own eyes and yet you tell me this–'

'You're speaking in riddles,' he replied. 'What have I told you? What is there you do not understand?'

'Oh, you know! You and Nicotte.' There! At last it was out.

'Nicotte!' he repeated. 'What in thunder has Nicotte got to do–?'

Susan hurried on, her words tumbling over each other as though she feared her ability to get them out.

'Oh, it's no use denying it,' she accused. 'I don't want to talk about it. I had proof – proof conclusive. I don't want to talk about that, though. It's too – too painful. All I ask you is to spare me any further humiliation until such time as you are free to do as your heart bids you.'

'I see.' Tearle nodded slowly, but his face,

as his words, was expressionless. 'So that's how the land lies.'

Despite his wife's announced conviction, it was evident she was waiting for him to defend himself, scanning his taut features with nervous eyes. The accusation was so unexpected it momentarily robbed him of speech. The fierce indignation which sought to find expression was checked by a surging up of his pride. She believed him guilty on the strength of her mysterious 'proof.' He saw no good reason to disillusion her. In the long run it might even assist in giving her complete freedom.

'You deny it?' she queried huskily.

'I'm not denying anything,' he replied. 'As for humiliation, shall we call it quits and close the account at that?'

The answer did not satisfy her. She had expected something more complete. There was reason even in her outraged pride. Had he confessed with some show of shame his love for Nicotte, she would have found a little sympathy for him, even though she eventually left him as she was determined to do.

'You might have told me,' she murmured. 'I – I should have tried to understand.'

'That's mighty generous of you.'

'Please don't mock me,' she demanded, testily. 'Credit me with some human feeling. From the very beginning this mad marriage of ours was doomed to failure. Now that the crash has come I want to shoulder my share of the responsibility. I ought never to have let you encourage me to think it could be otherwise.'

'You thought it could be otherwise then?'

'Of course. I dreamed all the dreams that come to girls who – who think they love a man. I started off with hopes, only to find them based on nothing. From the very beginning you deceived me.'

His eyes flashed angrily. To think she could say these things with such deep emotion when he knew the real hope that had been blighted, the hope that he was rich and that with his help she could maintain her friends.

'Don't hark back to that,' he growed. 'It's one of the things you ought to be glad to forget.'

'Yes, you're right,' she agreed, with rising anger. 'And I will forget it. I am going to find my happiness one day, as you've found yours.'

To her astonishment, he burst into mirthless laughter.

'Don't do that!' she snapped.

He shut his mouth like a trap and commenced to fling some wood into the fire. In this vicious circle of misunderstandings it was difficult to know which way to turn. She talked of humiliation – she who had humiliated him as no other man or woman ever had. She could even revive the past with a tear in her pool-like eyes. Truly she was amazing.

'Susan, you ought to go on the stage,' he said.

'Oh, you–!'

'I'm serious. You're sure the most beautiful and accomplished actress I've ever met.'

A sob came from her lips. It was the pressure of the two days' reaction. Another – one more, and then the breakdown. Her body trembled and rocked from her convulsive sobbing.

'Say, Susan!' At last Tearle was concerned. But she did not hear him. Everything was blotted out in that ocean of tears that seemed to pour from her very soul.

'Don't cry! For the love of Mike, don't cry!'

He was actually kneeling down beside her with her small hand held between his own, his twitching lips beating time to her heaving bosom.

'I guess you were right,' he confessed, his head wagging. 'I'm sure a bit of a brute at times. I never did understand women – not women like you.'

Her swimming eyes gazed for an instant into his, and the small fingers closed on the big hand. Then she remembered and swiftly hid her head and took her hand away.

CHAPTER EIGHTEEN

In the middle of the morning of the next day familiar noises from afar broke on their ears. Borne on the still air came the thud of axes, the humming of a saw and later a reverberating crash. It was like stepping out of a dream into a world of grim reality. They were at the point where the river merged into the lake. It was frozen almost completely, with only a single black line dissecting it where the strong current flowed, defying for a while the rigours of the frost.

'Tim-ber!'

The old cry came echoing through the trees and with it, Susan thought, came the sickly odour of fried fish mixed up with the equally overpowering smell of sap. Soon from out of the distance came the shack, looking like a doll's house amid the bigness of things. From the square wooden chimney escaped a coil of smoke.

'There must be someone inside!' she said.

'I left word for Nic – for a fire to be lit,' he explained. 'I guess it's best not to let them know what has happened.'

'But surely they must know – when you are not there?'

'They have a hunch I am ill,' he answered, with a little twisted smile.

'And I?'

'Well, naturally, you would be looking after me, wouldn't you? It was the best thing I could think of. In this camp there's little enough to talk about and other people's troubles make fine material for debate.'

She could appreciate his desire to keep the cause of his absence from the men. Yet someone must know the truth – the person who lighted the fire and spread the false news. She did not need to ask who that was. Nicotte was his confidante, his friend, his – his–

'Do you expect me to help in the cook-house again?' she asked suddenly.

'Not if you'd rather not.'

The answer surprised her. It seemed that he was not entirely lacking in consideration after all. To help Foo she would have to be near Nicotte. To expect her to accept that humiliating position was unnatural. She was glad he saw it in that light.

'Shall you move over to Shaggin's quarters?' she asked further.

'It's not worth while, I think. He may be back at any time. Do you particularly mind if I stay here?'

'Not in the least,' she replied with an indifferent air, but she could not forbear adding: 'But you understand, of course, that your – that Nicotte cannot–'

She saw the anger leap to his eyes, but he bit back his retort. They reached the shack a few minutes later, unseen by any of the workers among the timber. But Nicotte was inside, singing as she brushed the floor vigorously.

She swung round as the door creaked and dropped the broom in her agitation. Tearle merely nodded, and Susan, with pallid cheeks, stepped aside.

'You have good journey, yes?' asked Nicotte, the first to speak.

'Not so bad,' replied Tearle. 'Everything all right?'

Nicotte nodded and moved towards the door. She turned her eyes upon Susan and in them was a yearning. But Susan did not see it for her head was turned away.

'That's all, Nicotte,' said Tearle.

She went out and closed the door behind her. Susan, glancing through the window, saw her making across the snow towards the cook-house and was relieved to reflect that they would not meet often in the future.

As soon as he could Tearle went to see how things were going with the lumbermen. The sturdy Logan gave a wild whoop as he saw him coming and two sawyers sitting on their perch driving a saw through a six-foot fir stopped their labour to wave their horny hands.

'How are things, Logan?' greeted Tearle.

'Great. We've shure knocked hell out of thot forest. You're looking mighty fit for a sick man.'

'I'm not sick now.'

'What was it – influenza?'

'Something like that,' demurred Tearle.

He wandered across to the working gang and was pleased to see that Logan had not exaggerated. A gigantic amount of work had been accomplished during the past week. On either hand lay score upon score of logs which the indefatigable donkey-engine was hauling into the clear as fast as it could. Mat, the big Californian whom Tearle had worsted recently, trimmed off the last limb from a fallen giant and grinned good-naturedly.

'Guess we can cry "contract" this week-end, boss!'

'You're right. You've made *some* headway.'

'Wanted to show it ain't necessary to have a boss-logger at all. Is Shaggin coming back soon?'

'He ought to have been back before now.'

'Well, I won't be sorry. There's thirteen weeks' wages due to me. I tell you I'm sure crazy for a jag down west when I handle what's coming to me.'

'Tim-ber!' The cry rang out and Tearle gazed up to see the two sawyers in his near vicinity leap to the ground. The huge tree dipped her head and then with a crash

227

measured her length on mother earth.

'Big fellow that,' enthused the Californian. 'But we've found one away back which'll make that one look like a match-stick. When she comes down she'll sure go through the earth. How's Susan?' He changed the subject suddenly, chattering on: 'We sure missed her. That darned Chink has been serving up junk that ain't fit for a dog to eat. Gee, I've forgot what good grub's like. Tell her to cut out that fish for a bit. I'd sooner have bully.'

'You'd better talk to Foo,' said Tearle. 'He's going to run the show in future.'

Mat's jaw dropped before he swore roundly.

'Now ain't that jest cussed!' he growled. 'Here have I been working up a good appetite for the time when she'd quit nursing you. Say, can't you persuade her it's for the good of the cause?'

Tearle laughed and shook his head. Persuasion was useless, he knew, and he was of no mind to try it. He had seen the look which had passed between the two women in the shack and knew that war had been declared, war based upon a miserable misunderstanding.

As before, he found antidote to his troubles in work. To be with the men again was good. They at least were free from bickerings. They, like himself, took a pride in their work and were always cheerful when they were not engaged in cursing Foo, towards whom their antagonism was more apparent than real. During the day he worked out the timber and found he was within a few thousand feet of completing the big contract which Shaggin had undertaken.

With a view to celebrating such an occasion he rounded up Foo and went into the matter of provisions. Foo, who had a marvellous memory, rapidly detailed the various edible substances on his fingers.

'Good,' said Tearle. 'On Wednesday we are going to have a spread. The best meal you can dish up. You've got to beat all records, Foo. Cut out that dried fish and get busy with some traps in the lake. And I want that brandy.'

Foo's narrow eyes opened to their widest extent.

'No touchee spilits. Mistel Shaggin velly–'

'I'm running this,' retorted Tearle. 'Once in a while spirits are excusable. The boys have done the graft and they're going to have a picnic. Hunt up that brandy and put some pep into the cooking – and don't breathe a word.'

'Velly best!' promised Foo and mopped his moonlike face. The case of brandy which was kept for medicinal purposes was brought out from the stores and the Chinaman began to rack his brains for half-forgotten recipes likely to appeal to the palates of the lumber-jacks.

'Susan,' said Tearle that evening, 'will you do something for me?'

This unusual demand startled her, for she could not remember that he had ever before made a request of her.

'Well?' she asked.

'To-morrow I'm giving a kind of a party to the men to celebrate the completion of our contract. Foo really hasn't the time to do the thing alone and Nicotte knows nothing about cooking. Will you lend a hand?'

'Over there?'

He nodded and watched the look of indecision cross her face.

'I wouldn't ask you for myself,' he amended, 'but they are good fellows and deserve a little appreciation. Will you?'

'If you wish it.'

'Thank you!'

She went across the next morning, to Foo's delight, and commenced to plan weird and mysterious dishes. Two bottles of brandy were commandeered to make a tipsy cake which was a real innovation in that camp. She was making it when one of the men poked his nose round the door, drawn by the irresistible odour.

'What the blazes!' he ejaculated.

'Go away!' ordered Susan.

'Where'd you get that stuff – and what's in

the wind?'

At dinner-time the news leaked out. The men were like a lot of boys in their excitement. Anything out of the ordinary run of things came as a great relief from the monotonous life of the camp. Tearle explained briefly the object of the celebration and warned them that the brandy was good old-time spirit with a kick in it, and that thereafter there would be no medicine for any sick man. That prospect seemed to trouble them not at all, and after their midday meal they went out to battle with the timber once more.

Tearle had marked down the big tree which the Californian had mentioned as the last one of the day, the one which in actual fact completed the contract. All the camp turned out to see it felled, sliced and hauled into the clear.

A wild cheer went up as the keen saw worked its way down to the notch and the topmost branches moved ominously. With the first long 'crack' the sawyers leaped down. The mighty tree leaned and leaned until gravity brought it hurtling through the air to smash the small things in its path.

'Hooray!'

A deep-throated roar rang through the forest as the swampers leaped to their task. Axes gleamed in the sunlight under muscular and dexterous arms. The monster

231

quickly became as denuded as an earthworm, a mere collection of logs, ready for that rattling merciless donkey to play with.

Tearle, standing on the end of the biggest log, gave the word and the cable which held it went taut as it wound up on the drum of the ponderous machine. The log moved across the scarred ground and came up against a big stump. Tearle shouted to the donkeyman, but instead of slackening the cable grew tauter than ever. A hoarse shout went up from some of the watchers and Tearle leaped from the log and waved frantically towards the engine.

Then the thing happened while most were too dumbfounded to do anything but stand transfixed. The inch cable broke sheer at the coupling. With a vicious hiss it whipped through the air. Figures plunged blindly away from its line of flight. It was over in less than a second, but – lying prone on the ground, some twenty yards from the engine, was Nicotte.

'God, she's–!'

A dozen men ran forward, and the low growl from their throats was evidence of the seriousness of the catastrophe. Logan, as pale as death, jumped down from his platform.

'Something went wrong,' he cried hoarsely. 'I couldn't shut off. I tell you I couldn't shut off! Something went wrong.'

Tearle touched his hand.

'All right, Logan. We understand.'

Susan in the background could not see what was happening in the circle of male figures. She had never dreamed that anything like this could happen. Ignorant of mechanics and physical laws she had not credited the comparatively thin cable with this murderous strength. The crowd moved and Tearle came through it with the still body of Nicotte in his arms. The neck was swathed in improvised bandages and they were red – red–

A man went flying across to the stores for something and Tearle moved after him, carrying his burden as if she were a baby. His face was eloquent of his emotions. He felt himself partly responsible, and in that responsibility was agony unending. Had it been a man, one of those whose job it was to wage warfare with the forest, it would have been different, for the toll of the big timber was constant and men reckoned with it. But a woman!

'Is she – is she–?'

The man beside Susan stroked his beard.

'Maybe she'll win through, but–'

She gave a gulp and moved away from the scene. Whatever Nicotte might have been, all her sympathy went out to her now. In the presence of this dreadful thing there was no room for personal grievances. She prayed fervently that Nicotte might live.

CHAPTER NINETEEN

Of course, the accident put a stop to the contemplated banquet. It was cancelled unanimously and spontaneously by the men themselves. Much as they inclined towards festivity, sensitive hearts lay within those rugged breasts.

In the little room at the end of the big hut Nicotte lay dying. There was no doctor in camp, and even had there been one, he could have done nothing more than had been done. The cable had bitten deep into the small shoulders and neck, and the end was but a matter of time.

An hour after being taken to her room, she opened her eyes to see Tearle sitting by the bed. She started to speak, but he raised his hand to prevent her. She only smiled and went on.

'Did – you – bring me heer, yes?'

He nodded and caught the small hand in his.

'I understand,' she whispered. 'But you – must not worry, *mon ami*. Long ago time I t'ink I die in zee woods. I am ver' glad to die in ziss place.'

'Nicotte, you must not talk of–'

234

'But yet, I must. It is not mattaire much. I have ver' happy life – ver' happy life. My fader he die near heer – long time ago. Maybe I see heem soon.'

The red light of the declining sun smote through the curtain on to her pallid face, lending it a softness that was ethereal. Tearle went to lower the blind a trifle, but she stopped him with the slightest movement of her hand.

'I love zee sun – always he is my good companion. But of zee darkness I am ver' scare'. Will it be dark, *mon ami* – where I go?'

'I guess it will always be sunshine where you are,' he half choked. 'You've a brave woman, Nicotte.'

She laughed, but the movement of her muscles caused her to wince. Tearle winced, too, as if he also had felt the pain.

'Take my hands,' she whispered. 'In yours – so. Maybe Susan not mind now. No, she would not mind – now.'

The man's mouth twitched at the soft words and Nicotte's great eyes surveyed him keenly. Then she spoke, and he did not try to stop her, though she rambled on and on, slowly, sometimes almost incoherently, but always as though it eased her physical pain to lay bare her heart.

'I try to make you happy,' she began, her voice all but a husky whisper, 'jus' because you are so miserable. And you give to me so much pleasure, sweet pleasure like no other man. Always you are the good friend to me, and one time I nearly t'ink I love you. For why you turn your head away? Because I say that is it shameful? Oh, no, it ees jus' zee love I have for my brudder who go away many years ago and never come back. He look at me jus' lak you with beeg eyes that shine, and then I kiss him and he laugh.' For a few seconds she halted, as though for greater strength. When she went on, it was in a tenser tone: 'Someone love you ver' much and you do not know. She t'ink bad things of Nicotte – she t'ink– By Gar, I cannot tell you what she t'ink of me.'

'Nicotte, what are you saying?'

The girl's eyes grew hazy and closed, but the hands which held his so fondly were warm still. In the stillness of the hut his breathing sounded tremendous. The girl's long eyelashes fluttered and the tired lids opened again.

'Zere is no pain – I feel so happy.'

A knock sounded on the door, the mere tapping of a finger. Tearle gently released his hand and crept towards it. Logan stood there twisting his cap in his hand nervously. 'I've been waiting – waiting,' he groaned. 'Can't I see her? I gotta tell her something!'

A murmur from the bed was sufficient invitation for him. He pushed past Tearle

236

and dropped on his knees beside Nicotte. For a moment no words would come, but when they did they fell over each other in their haste to free themselves from the engineer's tortured brain.

'Something went wrong, kid. I'm telling you no man on this earth could have switched off the power. I tried – but nothing happened! She went on spooling the cable. Why, I wouldn't hurt a hair of your head! Didn't I bring them hairbrushes for your birthday? You don't think I was careless – it wasn't that. I saw that log jam and heard what the boss shouted – but something went wrong–'

Nicotte stopped the wild current of words by pulling down his head with a painful effort and kissing him on the cheek. A sob left his lips and he passed his sleeve across his eyes as he rose to his feet.

'I'd better go,' he said huskily. 'I promised the boys I'd go and tell them how things are.' He sank his voice to a whisper. 'Is – is she – pulling through?'

There was no need for Tearle to reply. His grim face was sufficient response. Logan sniffed and went through the door. A crowd of men awaited him by the bunk-house and he made known the verdict.

'Worse, you–!'

'Damn that engine,' he muttered savagely. 'If I had the man who made it here I'd – I'd–!'

'Well, what's done is done,' said another man, philosophically. 'It sure makes a fellow sick to see a gal go down like that, but it might 'a' been worse.'

Logan glared at him.'

'Yep, worse. It's bad enough, I'll allow, but that cable might have taken off half a dozen heads. The sapling broke its force and put it away from the crowd. I heered of a case where–'

Logan didn't want to hear it. He turned on his heel and hurried towards the woods, to try to find some mental rest. He was passing the shack when a voice hailed him and Susan came running across to him.

'Nicotte – how is she?'

'Bad,' he sighed. 'Guess she'll never see another sunrise.'

Tears of compassion sprang to her eyes. She had guessed that the case was serious from Tearle's failure to return and report to her. For the past hour her heart had demanded she should go and perform what service she could, but she had refrained on Nicotte's account. Nicotte would want to be with Tearle! Painful as the thought was, she forced herself to submission, and in this generous act of self-denial she found more comfort than she would have thought possible.

'Who is with her now?' she queried.

'Tearle. But I guess she'd be glad to see

you. There's nothin' like a woman to bring cheer to another woman.'

'I'll go,' she replied, and turned hurriedly towards the hut where lay the hurt Nicotte.

Reaching it, she knocked softly. A moment passed and then Tearle's head came round it. If he was surprised to see her, he concealed it.

'Can I see her, Douglas?' she whispered.

'Yes, but I think she is sleeping,' he whispered back. 'Unless—'

She shivered and tiptoed towards the bed. One of the French girl's hands lay over the blanket. Susan touched it and breathed more easily when she found it warm. Nicotte's eyes opened, but in the gathering gloom she did not at first recognize her visitor.

'It is I – Susan,' said Tearle's wife, softly.

'Susan!' The word left the trembling lips falteringly, then she added, with a smile that she forced through the lips twisted with pain: 'I prayed that you come. But I t'ink maybe somet'ing keep you. You have not speak to me for long time. I wish to speak to you – alone.'

She turned her eyes on Tearle, who read in them his dismissal and was quick to obey.

'Call if – if – you need me,' he admonished Susan.

She nodded. When Tearle had gone Nicotte breathed a deep sigh and asked that

239

the electric light be turned on. Susan switched it on and then, with a fluttering heart, drew a chair close to the girl's bed.

'To-night,' said Nicotte suddenly, 'I go on zee long trail.'

'No, no!'

'But yes – eet is so. Now I tell you some-t'ing ver' important. You heer what I say?'

'Yes.'

'You t'ink bad things about me many times, but eet is not true. And you t'ink bad t'ings about your husband.'

Susan waved her hands imploringly, but Nicotte paid no heed. Her one great last desire was to put things straight. Slowly, taking short, painful breaths between her words, she went on as inexorably as she had with Tearle, her great dark eyes begging for belief.

'At first I t'ink I love heem – yes, yes, zat is true,' she told her listener, and for a moment she stopped as though living again that time. 'Then he make me ashamed till my heart ache. I come heer and I cry and cry. Then I see I must not do this t'ing that I t'ink about – that he do not t'ink of me lak zat. And I t'ink of you, too, and I pray God will make me good.'

Susan felt, uncomfortably, that she should stop the girl, for her own sake, but there was that in Nicotte's earnest eyes that fascinated her and made her listen dumbly.

'He was so good to me,' went on the injured girl, plaintively. 'Jus' my dear beeg friend. He laugh at me and play with me, but never he forget you – never!'

Susan bit her lip, and hot tears filled her eyes.

'You do not believe me?' asked Nicotte, and she peered anxiously at Susan's face in the lamplight.

'Yes – yes, but–'

'Ah!' A nod emphasized the exclamation. 'I know. You t'ink of a day a week ago when you find somet'ing – eh?'

Susan moved uncomfortably and dashed the tears from her eyes.

'Wait!' whispered Nicotte. 'Now I tell you. Zat man, Conway, he bad man – dog. He come steal my stockings to make you believe dreadful t'ings that never were. I did not guess until you are gone away and then–'

Such a thing had never occurred to Susan. The significance of Nicotte's accusation stunned her.

'Nicotte, are you sure?' she begged, her own hand groping blindly for the hand on the coverlet.

'But yes. He come and speak to me while I am mending. Then I go away and when I come back I lose my stockings. Eet is true – true. You must see eet is true.'

Susan saw that now all too clearly. That she could have been so blind, so unimaginative, as not to have suspected some such plot amazed her. It brought her to such depths of shame and self-reproach that she knew not what to say. Doubting had gone to the winds. It only required one look into this dying girl's eyes to know that she could not lie. She burst into silent tears, great sobs shaking her body and rocking the rickety chair in which she sat.

'But you must not weep!' advised Nicotte.

'I – I can't help it. You make me so ashamed I cannot look at you. Nicotte, can you forgive me?'

Nicotte smiled bravely – the pain was now becoming greater than she could bear in spite of the soul-ease she had found – and her fingers trembled in Susan's hands.

'Zere is nussing to forgive,' she murmured. 'But I am so glad you come to see me – so glad. I t'ink you would not come.'

'I would have come before, but I knew my husband was here. I – I thought–'

She hesitated shamefacedly, but Nicotte was quick to understand.

'He nurse me because he is my good friend,' she defended. 'He bandage my wounds so tenderly. But eet is no good because all my blood is gone. Now I want to geev you somet'ing. Yes, yes – eet make me ver' happy if you take zem. Zere is my workbasket, a gold bangle my brudder geev me years ago. Maybe when you look at zem you remember Nicotte love you ver' much, and want you to be happy.'

It was plain that the sands of life were fast running out and must soon speed that brave spirit across the abyss. Susan's heart agonized as she saw the mass of bandages stained crimson. On the table beside her was a big roll of lint and a pair of scissors. Quickly she seized them to measure off a fresh dressing. Her hands gently touched the crimson bindings about the girl's neck, but Nicotte shook her head slowly.

'Too late!' she breathed, and a forced gasp sounded from her throat. Her head rolled to one side and her hands gripped the coverlet. The roll dropped from Susan's nerveless hands.

'Nicotte!' she moaned. 'Nicotte!'

Once more the eyes opened with a gigantic effort. Then they slowly closed for ever and a last plaintive sigh came from the half-open lips. In the terrible momentary silence the heart of Susan Tearle felt crushed between two slabs of ice. Gently, reverently, she pulled the coverlet over the dead face and crept from the room. She found Tearle in the shack gazing pensively into the stove, with an unlighted pipe in his hand. He looked up eagerly.

'Well?'

'She's – gone!'

Douglas Tearle's head bowed, and he held

his cap in his hand as he slowly walked away, wordless. She was glad when he was gone. She wanted to be alone for a while to regain her composure and to ponder her astonishing and painful revelation. She had made her peace with Nicotte whom she had so cruelly misunderstood, but there was still her husband. To tell him of her former terrible suspicion – nay, conviction – seemed impossible. To confess that she had thought him capable of the thing that had sent her off with Conway was out of the question. But (and the thought sent her cold) suppose Nicotte had already told him? But no, Nicotte would never have whispered that terrible secret to the man she had admired so much. Susan knew that now, knowing the soul of the dead girl as she had never known it in life.

New life, new hopes, came surging over her. All the nightmares were gone. Tearle was the man she had believed him to be. It was due to him that she should make some redress for this wrong she had done him. Love? Perhaps it was too late for that, but there was friendship, that thing which had transfigured poor Nicotte. There were companionship, sacrifice. Surely, surely she could make things better for him – and herself. She determined to leave nothing undone to prove she was worthy of his consideration; worthy of his friendship, of his confidence and of his respect. She wanted to be nothing smaller than had been Nicotte.

CHAPTER TWENTY

Even the passing of one as dearly loved as Nicotte, and through so tragic a means, could not long dampen the spirits of the men of the logging camp. Like children in so many other ways, they were, too, like them in the resilience of their emotions, and though their grief had been deep and sincere when they had laid away their girl comrade in the timber she had so well loved it had expended its greater portion on the day those rough primitive products of the wild had stood with bared heads in the resin tanged air and smothered the girl's grave with all the floral tributes they had been able to gather, far and wide.

Work, the panacea for all ills, and work such as was the life of such men, did its part in pushing the tragedy into the background and making it the memory that only time, in another environment, could have done. Day after day they went about their duties, and each day made the absence of Nicotte from her accustomed place in the dining-room a little less poignant; each day made them think more and more of themselves. It could not have been different, with the exuberant spirits of health and the tonic of work which was their portion.

It was when Tearle once again began to notice the restlessness of his men in the monotony of their lives, that he decided the time had come for the banquet which had been proposed for the night when Nicotte had left them, and which had been so long postponed.

It meant a vast amount of work and worry for Susan, but she went about it uncomplainingly and by evening of the day of celebration had succeeded beyond her expectations.

The meal was voted the greatest thing that ever happened and the tipsy cake 'the real goods.' Dancing followed, to the strains of a violin and a concertina. Naturally Susan was in great demand and before the evening was over had danced with every man in camp except Tearle.

At three o'clock in the morning she was still wondering why he had not asked her. That was the only flaw in an otherwise perfect evening. But even that was remedied before the party broke up. Logan, who danced like a professional and hungered for the chance to get another one in with the graceful wife of his boss, proposed a 'very last' waltz to close the programme. But before Logan had taken his first step with Susan, Tearle interposed his big figure and shook his head.

'No, you don't, Logan. It's about time I had a turn.'

'You got all your life to do it,' growled Logan.

'It's not wise to bank on that,' retorted Tearle. He turned to Susan with a whimsical smile. 'May I?'

She nodded and held up her arms, and they moved silently out on to the floor, jostled and bumped by the men whose steps were crude to say the least. Tearle danced well and looked as if he thoroughly enjoyed it. When the waltz was nearly at an end he whirled his wife past the orchestra and winked at the players significantly. They grinned and started all over again.

Susan could not help feeling pleased. It was new to her to see Tearle really letting himself go. He looked down and laughed at the sight of her reflective countenance.

'Tired?'

'No, I could dance all night.'

'You have done so. It's almost morning. There's Logan looking fierce. It's a shame, too, because he would make a much better partner than I.'

When the music eventually stopped he was genuinely sorry. This long-forgotten experience of holding Susan in his arms, of gazing into her eyes, of watching the joy engendered by the dance suffusing her cheeks was peculiarly satisfying. For a few beautiful minutes he had succeeded in forgetting things that were better forgotten.

The affair wound up with the forming of a large ring and the singing of 'Auld Lang Syne,' the ring revolving at ever-increasing speed until the last note was reached and the participants were almost completely exhausted.

'Three cheers for the boss!' called Logan.

They were given *fortissimo*, Susan joining in with the rest. Then she herself was cheered to the echo, and the laughing company slowly broke up and dispersed. She and Tearle stayed last to turn out the lights, after which they made their way across the crisp snow to the shack.

'It went off splendidly, don't you think?' she remarked.

'Fine! And it was all due to you.'

'Oh, no, not all,' she protested, but smiling, pleased at the praise.

'Sure. Without you it would have gone flat. A woman's a very necessary thing in a place like this. Men are all very well in their way. They'll keep things merry and manage to amuse themselves, but a woman brings in the better kind of feeling. Puts men on their mettle and stops 'em from being beasts.'

'I don't think those men could ever be beasts.'

'Maybe not, but they could be much less

than they are. I guess a woman's kind of leavening wherever she is.'

Such sentiments were a little astonishing coming from his lips. She had a suspicion than he was voicing them for her benefit, out of gratitude to her. Even so it was pleasant to hear, for she wanted to be of use – now.

She was up as early as he the following morning and had made up the fire by the time he came from his room. Now that Nicotte was no more she felt it her duty to carry on with the work of the camp kitchen until such time as some new arrangement could be made.

'Good morning!' greeted Tearle. 'You're about early.'

'There's such a lot to be done,' she explained. 'I've got to get the hut into order before breakfast. Are you still going on felling trees?'

'Sure. The men have got to be paid and fed whether they work or not, and Shaggin won't thank me to let 'em sit idle. He can trade all the timber he can cut. Coming over now?'

She nodded and went out with him into the keen, dry morning air. In the east the pall of night was beginning to lift, and a band of glorious light lay low down on the horizon. It filtered through the forest and touched the earth as if with angel fingers.

Stealthily it paled out the blazing stars and reached towards the west. Then the red rim of the big sun came over the brim of the earth and the world awoke.

The gong brought the men from the bunk-house on time, and the work of the day commenced. Now that the big contract was completed there was no occasion to work with the frenzy of the week before, and labour went on steadily enough, a ding-dong battle with the timber. When breakfast was served all traces of the banquet had been removed, and the energetic Susan was kept busy serving vast quantities of food and drink.

Despite the hard work of the previous day she looked as fresh as ever, and was as agile as a cat. There was a noticeable lack of the banter which Nicotte had been accustomed to, for it was only too obvious to the men that Susan was different. Despite the fact that they used her Christian name quite naturally, they regarded her in a different light. Nicotte had been like themselves part and parcel of the human machinery, but Susan was a volunteer. Their respect for her knew no bounds. Complaints were nil. They would have died on the spot rather than complain.

It was late in the afternoon when the long expected came to pass. Tearle, superintending the gang, heard from afar the pleasant tinkle of bells. He turned his head and a few minutes later saw a sled drawn by dogs emerge from the timber into the open. The driver waved the long-thonged whip and a faint 'Hel-lo' came on the wind.

'Shaggin!'

The guess was correct. The team broke across the open with loud 'woofs' and pulled up near the workers. Shaggin leaped down and ran towards Tearle.

'Gosh, it's good to be back! How-do, boys!'

He stood pumping Tearle's hand for quite a minute and then noticing the latter's glance at his hip slapped it hard.

'Nothing wrong there now. How's everything? By Jiminy, you've made a hole here!'

'We're through with the contract,' informed Tearle. 'This is all extra.'

Shaggin opened his eyes wide and shook Tearle's hand once more.

'That's *some* going. Well, I'll sure want every foot. I fixed up another deal while I was away back. Come over to the office and talk.'

They went there on the sled and, having given the dogs over to Foo to feed, sat down to discuss things in general. Shaggin's gratitude knew no bounds, but he was painfully shocked to hear about Nicotte.

'I'd brought her a present, too,' he said, shaking his head sadly. 'Well, it's no use kicking again' things like that. I guess accidents will happen as long as this old world lasts out, but it gets a man hard to see a gal go down. How's Susan?'

'She's fit. Taken over Nicotte's job.'

'Good. Now see here, Tearle, I got a proposition to make. How'd you feel towards coming in with me?'

Tearle stared at him and then shook his head slowly.

'Better think it over,' advised Shaggin. 'I'll give you a share in this outfit, and I'll build you a good house on the lake. There's enough timber hereabouts to keep me going for years to come. In the summer there's a steamer plying down the river. She'll take you to Vancouver in two days, so it ain't like being marooned. See here, I'll put you on a third share, and that means dollars.'

'It's no use, Shaggin, I'm hitting the trail tomorrow.' Tearle's answer had the firmness of finality.

'What!'

'That's so. It's mighty thoughtful of you to make that offer, but I can't take it.'

'Why not?'

'I've got a wife.'

'Well, can't she live here? I'm not expecting her to do any graft. I've got two Japs coming up next week. Don't turn down a chance like this, Tearle. Me and you can run this show like one-two. Don't say anything now – think it over.'

But the man might as well have tried to move the pyramids as to move Tearle. The coming of Shaggin had set in rapid motion earlier resolutions. At last Susan's husband was free to move towards the closing scene of a big chapter in his life. Susan should have her freedom without a minute of unnecessary delay.

'It don't need thinking over,' he said. 'Pay me what's due and trade me a tent and some grub. I'll be off at sunrise to-morrow.'

Shaggin, who had not for one moment anticipated this reception of his offer, scratched his head in perplexity, but he knew when a man meant 'no' and did not waste further words. To Susan, however, he mentioned it.

'So you're beating it to-morrow?' he asked her after his first greetings and expressions of gratitude.

Susan, who up to that moment had heard nothing about departure, was surprised.

'Did my husband tell you that?'

'Sure. I made him a generous offer and he refused it. He's the kind of man that's worth a mint of money in a business like this. See here, Susan, get him to change his mind.'

'I?' she asked, and the idea brought a humorous smile to her lips.

'Who else? Look, I'll put you up the dandiest kind of shack you ever saw; and damme, I'll furnish it, too. This place is as good as you'll find anywhere in the West. Will ye talk to him?'

'It would be no use,' she replied. 'He has made all his plans long since.'

'But you don't want to go, do you?'

'Yes; if he wants to.'

So Shaggin was forced to accept the inevitable. Susan saw no more of Tearle until he came to the shack late in the evening with a pile of provisions in his arms. On top of them was a seal-skin coat. He put the provisions on the floor and held up the coat.

'I traded this with Logan,' he explained. 'He got it from an Indian woman last fall.'

'But you can't wear that!' she remarked.

'I didn't get it for myself,' he said. 'I thought maybe it would fit you. Will you try it on?'

She slipped on the coat and found it fitted splendidly. The skins were in fine condition and the large skunk collar felt delightfully warm. He nodded his head approvingly and ran his hands over the sleeves.

'You'll need it,' he said. 'There's a cold snap coming. Let's see – tea, beans, canned pork, beef, matches, fruit, snow-shoes, rope–' He rattled off the articles and sighed contentedly as he realized he was replete in every respect.

'When are we leaving?' she asked, chiefly with the purpose of saying something.

'Sunrise. Nothing like getting away early. Shaggin gave me a new route down to Vancouver – the way he came back.'

'You're going straight there?'

The unexpected question made him glance at her swiftly. Strange she should ask that.

'Of course,' he replied.

'And then?'

'You ought to be able to get a ship back to England. Shaggin treated me generously – too generously, maybe. I'll have funds enough to buy you a passage–'

He halted as a low, quickly stifled cry escaped her lips. That he could talk so calmly of this parting hurt her deeply. Then she saw him bite his lip and the next moment realized to her chagrin that he had misinterpreted the interruption.

'It's your own money,' he explained stiffly. 'You earned it. Shaggin lumped the whole together – made it a round figure. He ought to have settled with you separately.'

She waved her hands despairingly. How could she make him understand that now her hurry to escape was not so great? How could she bring him to see that much had happened within her since poor Nicotte had engendered that feeling of shame in her breast?

'Susan!'

She raised her head.

'You're not going to fly off the handle again?'

'Do what?'

'Start the old wound aching afresh. See here, let's cut all that and make the most of this week. Let us be pals; and part pals when the time comes. Just because we make a hash of things in one respect it don't follow as a matter of course that we've got to hate each other.'

'Hate!' she ejaculated. 'I never—'

The sentence which might have meant so much was to go unfinished then, for it was cut short when Shaggin knocked and poked his head round the door.

'Anyone at home?'

'Come right in!' invited Tearle cordially.

Shaggin came in and sat down. He filled his pipe from the tobacco pouch which Tearle offered and then somewhat timidly announced the object of his visit.

'I – I had a little present for Susan. I planned to bring 'em across just now, but I reckoned you'd rather they stayed where they was. It's a handy little outfit for anyone taking the trail. I'd be happy if you'd accept them, ma'am.'

Susan laughed.

'I shall be delighted when I know what *they* are.'

'Why, that there dog-team, of course. It's no mortal use to me.'

'But–'

Shaggin waved his hand.

'They didn't cost me a cent,' he confessed. 'I gambled a fellow for them away back. Them dogs are sure huskies. They'll knock two days off the journey.'

Susan thanked him for his generosity, but the prospect of reducing the time by two days was not so pleasing as Shaggin evidently imagined.

'They're in the shed behind my office,' he said. 'And I've had a bag of pulped fish put up as "feed" for them. I guess you're pining to get away now. Well it's sure nacheral for a young married couple to want to be alone for a spell. Maybe you'll feel like starting a second honeymoon.'

He laughed vociferously, but neither Tearle nor Susan felt like joining him, and their echo was shallowly half-hearted had he noticed it. When Shaggin had gone Tearle sighed and smiled wistfully.

'A good fellow, Shaggin!' he remarked.

'Yes,' replied Susan cryptically. 'But like most men, obtuse.'

Tearle knitted his brow. The word was outside his vocabulary, and he failed to read into it the meaning intended. Which was rather a pity.

CHAPTER TWENTY-ONE

'Goodbye!' said Shaggin. 'You watch that second dog – he's got a habit of starting a fight. Gee, it's a great day to be making a journey.'

He gripped Tearle's hand and then Susan's. The gang of men in the rear of the sled clumped forward one by one to follow suit, each after his fashion. The dogs, anxious to depart, were raising a miniature inferno, the breath from their mouths going up like steam.

'Ready?' queried Tearle.

'Yes,' was Susan's answer.

'That offer's still open,' reminded Shaggin. 'Maybe I'll see you beating back one day.'

Tearle laughed, but shook his head. He waited until Susan had made herself comfortable amid the piles of gear and then raised the long whip and cracked it over the heads of the six dogs. The sled moved forward down the slight incline, gathered speed and sent a shower of stinging snow dust into the faces of the voyagers.

Susan turned and waved her hand to the crowd in the distance, but soon a bend in the trail hid them from view and Nature closed them in on all sides. Her first sensation of sled-riding was one of great elation. The silent, smooth movement was like nothing else on earth. The blood tingled in her veins and the keen wind was intoxicating as she breathed it deep down into her lungs.

'Wonderful!' she cried.

'Mighty welcome change after tramping it,' agreed Tearle.

'What do we do on steep up-grades?'

'Get off and push.'

'And downhill?'

'There's a brake. It bites into the snow and holds her pretty well.'

The landscape slid by as the powerful dogs pulled at the harness. Susan, sitting low, had a vision of waving tails and shaggy forms. Now and again the long whip cracked, but she noticed it seldom touched the dogs. The dexterity with which Tearle used the whip was marvellous. She could see the thong flip along the half-dozen backs and 'crack' a few inches from the whiskered nose of the big wolf-hound who took the lead.

'Where did you learn it?' she asked.

'What?'

'How to use a whip like that.'

'Dunno. I'm not a real dog-musher. You want to go farther north to find the breed.

I've seen a fellow pick up a flying bird with the thong. Here comes a bit that'll call for some aid.'

At the foot of the steep hill he halted the dogs and motioned her to get out. She took her place at the poles and together they pushed at the load, the dogs pawing the snow and panting loudly. At the summit the trail went winding away into the blue distance over slight undulations. The runners fitted into the impressions made by Shaggin on his recent trip, and the going was easy for some miles. Then rougher country was encountered and thereafter progress was reduced considerably.

Now and again they would come upon a well-packed trail whose surface was like glass. It evidenced the near existence of some town or settlement, the procession to and from which had beaten a highway across the white wilderness. But on the whole the route they followed was not an ideal one from the point of view of travelling surface, though according to Shaggin it saved some fifty miles in the long run.

'This is magnificent!' once more enthused Susan.

It was her constant cry throughout the day, and it was justified. She had imagined that a snow-bound country would become monotonous after a while, but this was far from the case. Every mile had something new to reveal. Every mountain top, every ravine, every patch of timber was different from the last. Swinging up the trail to the music of the bells was a joy one had to experience to appreciate.

'I never knew it could be like this,' she confided. 'One thinks of travel in snow and frost as something undesirable – something cold and bleak and generally unpleasant.'

'It can be mighty unpleasant when it likes,' replied Tearle. 'It was that day when Simpson–'

The reminder came like a stab of pain. Why did he recall that at such a moment as this? It was impossible to think of it without remembering all the other incidents associated with it – Conway and the terrible scene at Roaring Forks.

'Look! There's a wolf!' She was glad of the chance to change the subject.

'Making for the timber,' nodded Tearle. 'You can see them in dozens when you haven't got a gun.'

When at last the sun dropped away in the west and the intense cold of evening persuaded Tearle to call a halt, Susan was eager to start the business of camping. It was like old times again; those days that had seemed dull enough then, but were now gilded by the romantic glamour which time weaves about the most trivial happenings.

While Tearle went to cut firewood she

262

made an effort to get on good terms with the dogs, but with the exception of the leader – the big wolfhound – they seemed soulless beasts who snarled and quarrelled all the while they ate the food she distributed. The wolfhound was more domesticated – to the extent of taking food from her fingers more or less delicately.

'Have you got a name, dog?' she coaxed.

The great beast put his head on one side intelligently as if he knew he was being addressed by this extraordinary and beautiful thing. Encouraged by his friendly attitude she put out her hand and ran it over the thick fur on his back.

'Will you be pals with me?' she whispered, and put her head against his.

'Sure he will!'

She looked up and saw Tearle looking down with a whimsical smile.

'Do these dogs have names?' she asked him.

'You bet. I guess he's been called names you wouldn't care to repeat.'

'Don't be absurd! I mean real names – pet names.'

'Sure, but it would take you a lifetime to guess it. Maybe he's had a dozen names by this time, a new one every season.' He looked at the dog and shook his head. 'No, he ain't had that many, for he can't be more'n three years old.'

'How can you tell?'

'I was only guessing, but we *can* tell. Here, Whiskers, open your mouth.'

He inserted his fingers between the dog's teeth and pried the jaws apart.

'Three as near as anything,' he mused. 'But it was easy to tell he was young.'

'How?'

'Wants to be friendly.'

'But surely that's natural, even with a dog!'

'Yep, with a domesticated dog. With a dog who sticks to one master and gets to know him. These dogs – they're like merchandise and no man keeps 'em long enough to have any sentiment about them. They go from musher to musher and have half the flesh whipped off them before they reach middle age. Young Whiskers here has reached the stage when he begins to wonder whether it ain't foolish to expect anything from life except wallops, and cuss-words, and disappointment.'

Susan stroked the fine head of the dog and murmured a reproach at such destructive philosophy.

'It's horrid!' she cried.

'Maybe. But it's life. It gets humans that way, too.'

She stood up and faced him with reddening cheeks, astonished and hurt that he should have made such a rejoinder.

'Has it got you that way?'

264

'I'm like Whiskers – just wondering whether it's all worth while. Gee, that fire ain't burning well!'

He dropped to his knees before the smoking fire and fanned it into quicker life with his breath and by the use of his cap. Susan's quick anger diminished as she watched him. After all he might not have meant all she thought he meant. It had seemed to her that he was drawing a rough analogy between the conduct of the men who drove these dogs and her own towards him. Filled as she was with the worthiest of intentions such remarks seemed out of place; cruel.

Generously she strove to forget them, but they left her curiously silent during the meal which followed. When it was over and the remnants thrown to the still hungry dogs Tearle fished out his pipe with a sigh and rammed some tobacco into the bowl. He looked up to find her with a lighted brand in her hand and took it with a word of thanks.

'One day gone,' he mused.

'A day's march nearer home,' she quoted.

'Home!' He looked at her keenly. 'Susan, you'll be mighty glad to get there, eh?'

A long silence.

'Won't you?' he repeated.

'What do you expect me to say?'

'I dunno. But I reckon home-ties are pretty strong. I've never had a permanent home, so

265

it's a bit different with me.'

'Never had a home!' she ejaculated.

'Nope, I had a craze for wandering. No place has ever held me for more'n a year or so. But I had a farm once away east. I planned to settle there, but then the war came and, well, I just had to sell up and go soldiering. When at last I got free I felt pretty down and out. I wanted my farm back. I wanted to see my corn growing out there in the plains.'

Half humorously it occurred to Susan that what she was hearing was news to her – humorous, because she was this man's wife, and this was the first time he had ever spoken to her of his former life, now that he was sending her away from him. She looked away from him, wondering curiously if he would tell her more.

'Then why didn't you go back to it?' she asked.

'Money. There was trouble about my having a passage back. I had joined up in England and was discharged there. Oh, I had enough dollars to get back, but things were not too good in Canada and like a durned fool I planned to make a bit more so I could buy a farm. Snakes! It was like trying to raise barley in the desert. Well, I tried speculating with what capital I had. I was *some* speculator, I'll tell the world. I bought all kinds of useless things and sold them mighty cheap, but the fellow who traded it knew a thing or two. I guess it was like stealing candy from a kid.'

This led back to Lifton, far away Lifton where she had first known him. It brought back to her vividly that night when he had held her close to him and whispered words of love into her ear. It brought memories, too, of his queer behaviour just before and after their marriage. Who could have foreseen that it would lead to her sitting beside a campfire in the snowy wastes of Western Canada within a few days of final parting? She stirred uneasily as she permitted her mind to survey all that had happened since.

'Cold?' queried Tearle.

'N-no,' she stammered.

'I thought you shivered.' But when she did not reply he was quiet a moment as though in deep thought before he looked up, startled from his reflections at her question.

'What do you intend doing, after Vancouver? Have you thought it over?'

She had been wanting to put that question for some time, but only now summoned sufficient courage to do so. He took the pipe from his lips and gazed reflectively into the bowl of it.

'I hadn't thought much about it.'

'Does it mean so little to you?'

'What does it matter?'

'But it does matter. Douglas, I can't bear

to think of you wandering; homeless. Those lumberjacks seemed so much like human driftwood, doomed to wander on from camp to camp with never an anchorage. If our ways – lie – apart, I want to feel that you are getting the best out of life. This country is wonderful enough. This free life under the skies has its fascinations, but there must come a time when – when a man like you will want the things he was meant to have–'

'What things?' His eyes seemed to bore into her as he asked the simple question. And his words, cold as the ice that sparkled from the thorn tree branches about them, left her shivering. She was chilled to her soul, and she was dumb. What could she say to him without laying bare her heart!

CHAPTER TWENTY-TWO

The glorious weather held. Each morning found the sky free of cloud and the air still and exhilarating. The trail had led the wanderers through a veritable wonderland of sunshine and shadow across frozen rivers and lakes, over mountain tops, always westward. To give Tearle a change Susan had taken to mushing the dogs, and had found that vocation even more pleasant than being a passenger.

She had christened all the dogs, but had not succeeded in making friends with any but Whiskers, whose infatuation for her was unmistakable. For the first time in his life Whiskers basked in the sunshine of human affection, and it was much to his liking. When the rest of the team were curled up in the snow fast asleep from their strenuous day, Whiskers would walk across to his mistress and poke his nozzle into her hand, or lie down before her with his luminous eyes regarding her fixedly.

'He's your slave all right,' laughed Tearle.

'Perhaps I have succeeded in convincing him that life is worth while after all.'

'Maybe; but don't spoil him.'

'Spoil him! Why should it spoil him to be treated decently?'

He did not answer, but Susan could not help noticing that whenever she fondled Whiskers her husband was a little cynical. She had a sneaking idea he was envious. Yet Tearle, too, was fond of the dog.

'I am sure he loves me more than he does you, though,' his wife protested mischievously.

'That's natural.'

'I don't see why.'

'I'll lend you a mirror, then.'

She blushed at the unexpected compliment. It was not often he indulged in flattering remarks.

'Do you know what to-morrow is?' she queried.

'Friday.'

'Yes, but what else?'

'I don't know.'

'Can you have forgotten? It is New Year's Day. Are you framing your good resolutions?'

His eyes came up until they met hers squarely. One other thing he had not forgotten, and that was the close proximity of their goal. By noon the next day he hoped to be in Vancouver.

'What kind of resolution can a fellow like me make?'

'I don't know. Surely there must be some worthy resolve left to you?'

'A whole lot. I could give up drink, or tobacco.'

'You are not addicted to drink, and as for tobacco, that would be a useless sacrifice.'

'What else is there, then?'

'I know something,' she murmured.

'You might drop me a hint.'

She hesitated, fearful of giving voice to the word which hung on her lips. He sat watching her in stony silence.

'It's your – your pride,' she stammered.

He laughed scornfully.

'I mean it,' she said, and what she said ended with a plea in her tones. 'Your pride obstructs your reason. When it suffers a jolt you get as stubborn as a mule. You let it blind you to realities. Douglas, don't let it blight your whole existence.'

'Well, that's news to me,' replied the big man. 'Up to a point you're right. But after that you're wrong. It ain't pride that hurts; it's failure.'

'What failures have you to worry about? You've won through hardship and trouble–'

'Oh, that!'

'Don't – don't be so disparaging. What has changed you since last summer? You remember that evening at Lifton, and the days after, when everything seemed so promising. There was something about you then that was different. The change is so subtle I can't describe it.'

'What change?'

'In your attitude towards things – towards me,' she blurted out. 'There seems nothing to account for it, for you break out with a cruel remark. I've watched you and it hurts me to think that things have come to this pass. And this talk of failure. What failure?'

It was the first time for months that any conversation had developed along these lines. But to-morrow Vancouver would be in sight with all its grim significance. Most of her own pride had gone now! With all her heart she desired some kind of rehabil- itation, if it were only a resumption of the present unnatural existence. At least that might develop into something – in time. Parting meant the end of all things.

'The failure ought to be sun-clear to you!' he remarked, and there was a return of the grim lips tightening that had for a time been absent. Memory was again jogging Douglas Tearle. 'Isn't it?'

'N-no. Has it been all failure?'

'You know it has. What are we – you and I? A mock wife and a mock husband, both living a lie.'

She shrank into herself at the merciless retort. He saw it and remorse came.

'I guess I do say some hard things, Susan,' was his confession. 'Maybe I could put the same sense into softer words. But it's true, and nothing can alter it.'

272

'If it's true,' she asked hoarsely, 'how did it come about? What made you treat me as you did at the beginning? Why did you not come to me and tell me you were poor – that you intended dragging me to Canada? Why did you make promises you never had any intention of keeping? It was then we were alienated, and ever since that alienation has loomed up like a skeleton to darken the sun. Why did you do it?'

His brow furrowed with astonishment. Her voice, her actions all combined to evidence her innocence. Only damning fact remained to prove she was acting, though for what reason he could not understand. In the circumstances there was little cause to hide her former duplicity. The only possible cause could be that she was ashamed to remember it. But that made matters no better in his eyes for, while willing to take his full share of the responsibility for all their unhappiness, he considered that the first move towards an atmosphere of truth should come from her.

'It's a mighty queer question for *you* to ask,' he said meaningly.

'What on earth do you mean?'

'Think!'

'I am thinking. I've been thinking these past six months. What have you on your mind? And why do you look at me like that?'

'You sure are a riddle,' he muttered, and

relapsed into a silence that nothing would break.

Tortured by her painful thoughts she sat by the fire long after the darkness came down. Occasionally she glanced at her husband to find him deep in obviously painful reflections. It became increasingly difficult to understand him. He had taunted her about their unnatural partnership and yet it was he who laid down the conditions. On the very night of the wedding it had started. Then there was that incident in the lumber camp when he had deliberately nailed up the communicating door. The blood mounted to her cheeks as she thought of these things. They had militated against the natural inclinations of her heart; damped them down by the ignominy. What did he expect – that she should go down on her knees before him and plead for love? No, that was not his motive. Hard as he appeared to be, at times she saw in him so many splendid traits. Whenever she attempted to blame him the fineness of his character came to level the balance. He was much like a man with a storm raging in his bosom, a storm which time had not succeeded in quelling. But why – why – why?

'I am tired,' she murmured at last. 'I think I will go to bed.'

He raised his head and gazed at her keenly.

'We shall hit Vancouver to-morrow.'

'I know,' she replied softly, pausing at the flap of her tent to gaze wistfully, first at the far horizon, then back at her brooding husband.

'You'll be glad?' A mere lifting of his eyebrows.

'I – I ought to be glad. Are you?'

'If you are,' he relied enigmatically.

'I'm not sure,' she said slowly, watching him steadily.

'No matter.'

'Whatever happens, you know, we shall still be husband and wife.'

'The law can alter that – if you wish,' was his blunt comment.

'Di-divorce?' she quavered.

He nodded. 'You can bring suit against me where and when you like. You have all the proofs you need.'

He spoke without bitterness, as if it were a fact that left no room for denial on his part. But it brought from her lips a strangled sob.

'Why do you say such things?' she cried. 'You know that's not true.'

'But you said so yourself. Wasn't that why you went away – with – with–'

'No – no. At least – I – I–'

'No need to worry about it now,' he said calmly. 'If you care to bring that against–'

She turned her indignant eyes upon him and stamped her foot as she flared out at him.

'It was all a terrible mistake. Nicotte told me so herself! But I ought never to have believed it for a moment! Do you think I haven't suffered for that misunderstanding?' she cried. 'Those stockings, that caused the trouble, were stolen by that awful man and hidden in your room. Wasn't it natural for me to–?'

As realization of what she was saying, what it meant, slowly broke over him, Tearle's face lost its habitual calm. His big hands closed and unclosed as the truth was borne in.

'The skunk! The low-down, dirty cur!' was his exclamation, and those sinewy hands seemed almost to feel the neck of the man of whom he spoke.

'And you – you believed it?' he accused. 'I'm no angel, Susan, but this – this–!'

Alarmed at the passion she had aroused, Susan sought to soothe him.

'Don't think of it any more, please,' she begged.

But Tearle did not answer. He feared what he might say.

He struck a match savagely and lighted his pipe. Susan shifted the blanket on which she had been sitting and lifted her tent flap.

'Good night, Susan!' he said, but his tone was altered.

Inside she lighted the candle and prepared to settle down for the night. It was not advisable to remove more clothing than was absolutely necessary. She took off the sealskin coat and gum-boots, slipping on a pair of moccasins in place of the latter. Then she let down her mass of hair and started to brush it vigorously. It crackled in the cold, dry air and rippled like gold as she shook it free from her head. Brushed, she fashioned it into two long plaits which fell far below her waist.

But despite her fatigue, sleep would not come. How could she sleep with to-morrow ticking its way ever towards her? Outside was Tearle facing the same crisis. What were his thoughts? Was he really as indifferent as he pretended to be? Did he only remember the friction, the bickerings, the unhappy moments of the past? Was he blind to other things, those admittedly rare occasions when a better spirit had existed? Had he forgotten that once he had taken her in his arms and kissed her? Had there been another woman in the offing she could have understood it, but as matters stood, his actions and resolutions were unfathomable.

She turned and twisted on her rough bed in a confused state of mind until at last she threw the blankets aside and rose. A low voice came from outside, a crooning voice which caused her to wrinkle her forehead in surprise. She crept to the tent opening and pulled aside the flap. Tearle was sitting by the fire in the same attitude as when she had left him. By his side was Whiskers, the dog, sprawled out flat, with his nozzle in Tearle's lap.

'All over, boy!' murmured Tearle. 'I guess I'm going to be lonely – lonely. Hell! Why did I do so mad a thing? You're wondering what it all means, eh? Well, I kinder see your argument. She's sure a looker! Full of pluck, too; full of life. Why worry? But that is the rub, Whiskers. Once a fellow starts a thing he has to see it through though it lays him out stark and stiff.'

Susan's heart-beats quickened in her bosom. Could a woman's intuition fail to read things between the sentences? He was afraid of to-morrow, even as she was. He would be lonely – as she would be. Then why – why suffer this inexcusable thing? Already it was past midnight. The New Year was in. Oh, to wash out all the miseries and misunderstandings as easily as time washed out time!

For apparently no reason Tearle turned his head and started as he saw his wife standing there with the light of the fire on her oval face. His caressing hand left the dog.

'Can't you sleep?' he asked.

'No. I – I've been thinking.'

'So have I.'

'About to-morrow?'

'About to-day.'

She moved towards the fire and stood close to him, so close that one of the hanging plaits of hair touched his face. He caught it in the ends of his fingers and retained it. She felt the slight touch and turned her head.

'Douglas, are we doing the right thing?' she asked, and the pleading tone held much of tenderness.

'I don't know. I wish I did.'

'Then–!'

'Then what?'

'People need not go on making mistakes for ever, need they?' she added meaningly.

Her eyes shone with the reflected fire of her emotions; great liquid pools filled with the light of reasoned love. The hand which touched her hair moved up until it rested on her shoulder, and when the man spoke his voice was vibrant.

'You mean some other way than parting?'

'Yes. Partings are cruel and so often regrettable. Are we past all understanding of each other?'

In this, what she believed her final appeal, she was humbling herself to bring him across the ocean of unfathomable prejudices. Nor was her appeal vain, for she saw his face lined with indecision, vague doubting.

'D'you know what you are saying, Susan?'

'Yes, yes. We're nearly at the cross-roads, Douglas. Another step and it may be too late.'

'Too late!' he muttered. 'God, I know that! I have thought of it till my head is bursting.'

She smiled wistfully.

'Isn't it time to do more than think?' she queried, pointedly.

'Yep. You're right. If–'

'Is there any "if"?'

'There seems always an if between what one wants and the getting of it. If there wasn't any past–!'

Her hand moved out and caught his. It brought them even closer together. His free arm moved as if it would encircle her and crush her to him, but it hesitated and waved impotently.

'Is the past such a spectre as all that?' she whispered. 'Just because we have been estranged, unhappy, at war in our hearts in thoughtless and unforgiving moments, must we let such times rob us of our future?'

'Susan!'

'Douglas! Let us forget!'

On the verge of giving way before this almost irresistible call to love the old canker began to operate.

She saw the mouth close tightly and knew the microbe of trouble, whatever it was, was at work again.

'Does it mean you can't – can't forget?' she stammered.

'You've guessed it! I can't. Maybe I'm crazy, but isn't there something you haven't told me; something you did that – that wasn't on the level – No, I don't mean Conway,' as if reading her thought, 'I mean – er – something you did before you married me.'

'Before I married you!' she gasped. 'You've no right to ask that – no right–' Indignation overcame all other emotions. She would not go on.

'Think – think!' he pleaded.

But she had thought quite sufficiently. She saw in his intimation nothing but vulgar inquiry into her single life; a doubting of her honour. It sent the angry blood rushing through her veins. After all she had done to wash away obstacles, to bring about such peace as her soul pined for, he had considered it opportune to put an insulting question no man had a right to put. She recoiled from him.

'Susan!' One hand went pleadingly towards her.

'Go away!' she screamed passionately. 'I hate you– Oh, how I hate you!'

He stood like a statue until she disappeared into the tent to lie and wait for the dawn – and the future.

CHAPTER TWENTY-THREE

Dawn found an outraged couple making ready for the last stage of their journey. To Susan the world was in ruins. Everything seemed ugly and mean; even the dawn which came up in splendour and sent the shadows scuttling away down the mountains. To think that was the question which had been rankling in his mind all those months – some dreadful groundless suspicion unworthy of the lowest of men. Ugh!

They ate their breakfast in silence, cleared up, packed the sled, harnessed the dogs and started off. For several hours no words passed between them. She was not aware that he was driving the dogs unmercifully as if Vancouver was some Paradise which he was anxious to see without a moment's delay.

At noon they arrived at a township. It was little more than a collection of scattered houses, a store or two and a decent hotel, but it was on the C.P.R. and the station was noisy with traffic. The team was pulled up in the main street and Tearle went into the hotel to get some tobacco.

'How far is it to Vancouver?' asked Susan of a passer-by.

'Matter of fifteen miles. Half an hour by train.'

She thanked him and waited for Tearle. He had evidently been making similar inquiries, for he looked at the dogs and hesitated.

'Have to get rid of this outfit,' he remarked at length. 'There's no snow yonder.'

'Do you mean to stay here?'

'There's a train this afternoon and another this evening. Better have a meal here and catch the afternoon train.'

'But what about the dogs?'

'They'll buy 'em at the store lower down the street.'

Susan reflected on the matter while they ate the welcome meal which the hotel provided. If there was no snow on the western side it was obviously impossible to take the sled farther. To dispose of it and the dogs became a necessity.

'I won't sell Whiskers,' she said. 'I want him – to keep.'

He nodded silently. Later they went to the store and bargained with the proprietor. He turned up his nose at the team and made an offer for them exclusive of Whiskers which Tearle laughed at.

Eventually the deal was clinched and Susan found herself in possession of a fair sum of money. But it was questionable whether it was sufficient to get her home in comfort, and she was determined to take nothing from Tearle.

Half an hour before the train was due to start Tearle came into the lounge with his belongings neatly packed. It was obvious that he intended to accompany her, but she preferred him not to.

'Do you want to go to Vancouver,' she asked, 'to see me off?'

'Why not?' he nodded, but her head shook with decision.

'It is better to say good-bye here,' she informed him with dignity. 'There may not be a boat sailing for some time. You said you hated Vancouver.'

'But–!'

'Let it be here – please!'

She was striving to suppress her emotion. She was determined that, come what might, she would never – no, never – again give this man any inkling of her true feelings. But, even now after what had been said the night before, the old reluctance came swimming in. So she wanted to get the business of parting over with the least possible delay.

'Very well,' he replied heavily. 'I got some dollars of yours. You'll need them.'

'No – no!'

'Eh!'

'I couldn't touch your money.'

'It's not mine. Half of it is–'

'I won't have it.'

'You can't get a steamer ticket to England with what you have. Susan, be sensible.'

'Sensible! I'm sensible enough. I shall cable my uncle from Vancouver. He will send what is necessary.'

He gulped, but did no more urging. When a little later he paid the bill, he intimated that it was time to start for the station. Whiskers, free of his harness and as merry as a kitten, ran beside his mistress, his high spirits entirely out of harmony with hers. Tearle saw her safely inside the train and waited outside for the whistle which would send her moving out of his life. She came to the window at the last moment and leaned out.

'Good-bye, Douglas!'

'Good-bye, Susan!'

An awkward pause during which he almost crushed the hand she offered.

'I'm – I'm – sorry–'

A whistle blew and the train gave a jolt.

'Douglas, where are you going?'

'Up there – among the timber. Good-bye!'

'Good-bye!' she quavered. 'Goo – goo–!'

But he did not hear the sob that completed the word. It was all over. Peering from the window with the unbidden tears wetting her face she saw him standing where she had left him, erect and imposing still, but a lonely man. Then a bend in the road hid him from view. She fell back into her seat and let her tears come. Whiskers, divining that something was amiss, jumped up beside her and pawed at her arm.

'Oh – oh!' she sobbed. 'Why did I let him go?'

By the time Susan Tearle reached Vancouver, however, there was little outward sign of her inner feelings. Coming out of the wilds after six long months of isolation the noises and sights of a city deafened and bewildered her. She was aware, too, that her clothing was no longer suitable and that the first thing to do was to invest in a wardrobe sufficient to last her until she reached England.

After booking a room at an hotel she sallied forth to purchase the necessary things. Prices were high compared with England, and by the time she had finished half of her funds had gone. It brought her to the question of passage money. Uncle Peter was her only hope. If Uncle Peter failed her other means would have to be adopted, but exactly what means she had not stopped to consider. There was one thing, however, that her months in the wilds had taught her: an independence such as she had never before dreamed of. She knew, as she had never known in England, that Susan Tearle could take care of herself; could work at anything. And she felt none of the fear of new enterprise that would have assailed Susan Lessing.

She composed a cable in terms calculated to soften her irate relative's stony heart and sent it by the quickest route. Of course the last time he had refused her point-blank, but she hoped that he might appreciate the position in which she was placed.

Two days passed with no reply. In the meantime she had made inquiries about a boat and found that one was due to leave six days hence. On the morning of the third day a cablegram was brought to her after breakfast. It was a lengthy affair and in addition to informing her that two hundred pounds had been cabled to a bank in the city, apprised her of the death of Uncle Peter three months before. It begged her to come to England at once since her uncle had died intestate and she was next of kin. It was signed Jones & Jones, Lincoln's Inn Fields.

'Well!' said Susan Tearle, and she laid the cablegram down beside her plate and calmly finished her pancakes.

But in spite of her repression, the news was something of a stunner. She had seen too little of her uncle to feel any deep emotion at his death. She remembered him only vaguely, as a crotchety, ill-tempered man with violent prejudices and miserly temperament. Nevertheless, she strove to feel sorry, but without any great success, as she would have been compelled to admit.

One thing was certain. She would never be in need of money again. She knew enough of Uncle Peter's affairs to be certain that he left a considerable estate. Now all of it would be hers! Singularly enough, though, apart from the momentary relief which the news afforded, she experienced no great elation. There were greater things in life than money, she had come to know. And she had missed the greatest.

At the bank she found everything in order. The production of the cable was sufficient to give her immediate possession of the money sent. She wired back to Jones & Jones informing them that she was sailing on the next boat.

For the first time in a long time her thoughts turned to Peg and Edith far away in Lifton. She wondered how they had managed to get on in her absence. She imagined their joyous surprise when, without warning, she would step into the little cottage there, if, indeed, circumstances had not forced them to leave it. But even the thought of a resumption of the old carefree life brought no pleasure. Everything seemed strangely hollow. The ideals, the ambitions which had burned so fiercely a year ago were no longer attractive. She would paint again, she would doubtless do good work, but–!

'What is it that has changed me, Whiskers?' she whispered. 'I'm not the same woman. It's just as if someone had taken the soul out of me and gone away with it.'

Whiskers looked at her with his intelligent eyes. She kissed him fondly. He was the only link with the immediate past. To look at Whiskers was to remember Tearle, and to remember Tearle was painful and pleasant at the same time.

'Did he ever love me, Whiskers?' she queried. 'Do you think he ever loved me at any time?'

'Woof – woof!'

'You darling to say that, but I can't believe it. He left me – let me go away. No! He drove me away with an accusation that was – beastly. Why did he do that? You don't know; no more do I.'

She liked to confess her inner feelings to Whiskers. It was a gigantic relief to her pent-up emotions to have something to confide in, and Whiskers was the only safe confidant she possessed. Besides, it helped some just to hear the sound of her own voice.

The days dragged along and she began to pine for departure. On the day before the boat was due to sail, she was reading the local newspaper when her eyes fell on a paragraph which arrested her attention. In a motor accident the previous evening a young man named Daniel Mainwaring had been knocked down and injured. But it was the concluding sentence which caused her to utter a cry of pleased surprise. It informed her that the injured man had but recently arrived from England to take up a post on the staff of that journal.

'Dan!' she exclaimed. 'What a coincidence!'

It followed naturally that she should call and see him to condole with him on his ill-luck. At his office, she was given his address, and a quarter of an hour later she was ringing the bell outside the house. She gave her name and after waiting a few minutes was shown upstairs. Mainwaring with his head in bandages and with excited eyes was sitting up in bed.

'Susan!' he cried, exultantly.

She took his hand and sat down beside the bed.

'This is extraordinary!' he ejaculated.

'It is, but how are you?'

'Oh, I'm all right – only bruised and cut about a bit. But how did you know I was here?'

'I saw it in the newspaper and called at their office. They gave me your address. So you've given up freelancing and taken a permanent post?'

'Yes– But tell me about yourself. I had no idea you were out here. Are the other girls here too?'

'No. They are still at Lifton. At least they were when I left. But surely you knew I was in Canada?'

He shook his head vigorously and gazed at her keenly.

'Didn't you see Edith or Peg after I left?'

'No. I wrote to you when I heard I had got this job, but the letter was never answered. Didn't you get it?'

'No. I dare say it is following me round.'

Mainwaring's attitude puzzled her somewhat. In spite of his evident pleasure at seeing her, he seemed to have something on his mind. She noticed that his hands played nervously with the counterpane on the bed.

'Am I worrying you?' she asked.

'No – no! Why, of course not.' But he hurriedly went on to other things. 'Susan, what happened after I went away from Lifton? Did that fellow Tearle stay on?'

The blood mounted to his visitor's cheeks, and she winced visibly.

'So you don't know – even that?' she asked slowly.

'Know what?'

'I – I married Tearle.'

Mainwaring's astonishment was undeniable, incredulous.

'You married Tearle, you say!'

'Yes, but why–?'

'Susan, you're jesting?'

291

'Why should I jest in so serious a matter?' she asked, somewhat tartly.

'I see,' he muttered. 'But it's extraordinary, all the same. Did he bring you to Canada?'

'Yes.'

'And you're living here in Vancouver?'

'No. I only arrived here a few days ago. But don't ask me any more, please. Do let us talk about something else; something more pleasant.'

Mainwaring was silent for a minute or two, but his curiosity impelled him to speak again.

'Didn't it turn out happy, Susan?' he begged softly.

A slight tremor passed through her and she shook her head.

'I see,' he nodded, understanding. 'I see! And you've left him. That's it, isn't it?'

And in the face of unexpected sympathy Susan Tearle found all her repression melting away. Then she let herself go, as she burst out with her full confidence.

'Yes – yes. From the very beginning it was a failure. Something crept in to ruin everything. And to-morrow I am going back to England – to forget.'

She turned her head to try to hide her deep emotion from him, but he had seen it, and his agitation noticeably increased. He opened his mouth to speak, but closed it again as if he were afraid. It was still unsaid when Susan rose.

'I shall have to go now,' she told him. 'I am so glad you are not hurt much. Write to me sometimes, Dan. I shall be glad to hear from you.'

The young man put out a detaining hand.

'Wait!' he begged.

'Why, is there–?'

He leaned across the pillow with an enigmatical expression in his eyes.

'Susan, you know I – I loved you once? Oh, you needn't be afraid, or angry! I'm not going to harp on that broken string. It's because I loved you I want you to be happy. Be frank with me. Do you still love your husband?'

'No.'

But the answer did not satisfy him.

'You're sure?'

'I – I– Oh, Dan, what are you asking me? I ought not to love him; I ought not to think about him, but I do. In spite of his strange and harsh conduct at times he is the best and finest man I ever knew. Yet I can't understand him–'

'I can.' Mainwaring's teeth clamped grimly down on the words.

'What do you mean?'

'I am the cause of this, Susan,' he confessed as calmly and as bravely as he could. 'I did something in a moment of mad jealousy which I believe brought about this tragedy.'

'How – how could you?'

'Before I left Lifton I saw you were in love with Tearle and I knew he loved you. I couldn't understand it then. He was so different from you – from any of the people you knew. I could understand his love for you. That was genuine enough.'

'So was mine for him,' she cried.

'Was it? Susan, one evening at Lifton I found a diary belonging to Peg. I didn't know it was a private book until I opened it, and then I saw something which took my breath away. It was about Tearle and about a pact made between you and the other girls. Peg had it all there–'

A strangled cry left Susan's lips as the blood left her face ashen pale.

'Yes – yes,' she cried, remembering. 'We did that! But it was before I fell in love with Douglas. When I found that I loved him, I repudiated that despicable arrangement. Before I permitted him to make love to me I told them that I would have no more to do with it. Dan, I have forgotten it – completely forgotten it.'

'But he hasn't.'

'He! You mean – you mean that Douglas knew – that?'

Dan turned his head from her searching eyes.

'Dan! Dan! You didn't mean that?' Susan's voice rose hysterically.

'I told him,' muttered the man on the bed, his face still turned from the woman to whom he confessed. 'Perhaps it was mere jealousy; perhaps it was because it didn't seem honest to trick him. Anyway I told him before I left. I showed him the book itself, because he called me a liar and looked like murdering me.'

The light of the world went out. Susan Tearle was crushed. At first her brain seemed to refuse to function; then, with bewildering suddenness, thoughts tumbled over each other with their painful cleaning effect. She could see now why Dan had been surprised at the marriage. Everything was clear as clear could be. Tearle had married her out of spite, that she might be hoist by her own petard. When love had come to him later, as she believed it had, he had choked it down because of his knowledge of that plot. All the queer talk and strange conduct on his part was accounted for.

'Susan. Can you forgive me?'

At first she seemed hardly to hear the pitiful, pleading voice of her one-time wooer. When, finally, it sank into her what he was saying, pleading for forgiveness, a twisted little smile played about her mouth.

'I find it more difficult to forgive myself

for ever entertaining so miserable a plot,' she finally told him. 'What must he have thought of me! Oh, I can't bear it.'

'You must, Susan. It isn't too late now.'

'Yes – too late.'

'No. You've got to tell him. Even though you come back again you've got to clear yourself. You can't let him go on thinking that. In the interest of Truth itself he should be told. Don't you see it that way?'

'Yes,' she murmured. 'He ought to know – he ought to know.'

'Then go find him. He can't be far away.'

'I'll find him,' she promised, and it was her last speech. Wordless, she lifted Mainwaring's hand in a silent goodbye as she left to keep that promise.

CHAPTER TWENTY-FOUR

After the first crushing blow Susan found elation filtering through the storm clouds that had encompassed her. At least there would be no more misunderstanding. To find Tearle became an obsession that brooked no delay. She left Vancouver within an hour, headed for the place where she had left Tearle.

But to her disappointment, if not her surprise, he had left the township. From the dealer to whom they had traded the dogs and sled, she bought them back at a considerable loss. Two hours later she had the team harnessed, with Whiskers at the head of it, and such provisions as she might require securely lashed aboard.

Though there were more important things than Jones & Jones of Lincoln's Inn Fields, she remembered to cable notifying them of the postponement of her departure. That Tearle had been as good as his word and made tracks for Shaggin's camp she was convinced, but whether or not he would take the trail by which they had arrived was not so certain. That, however, was not an important matter since his objective was fairly evident.

She set off in the dusk of evening and soon left behind all trace of civilization, nor did she stop until the need for food and warmth became urgent. She made her camp in a sheltered spot and there was grateful to find the remains of a fire. It might not be Tearle's fire, of course, but her heart told her it was, and her spirits rose many degrees.

She had imagined that she would feel afraid camping alone in the wilds, but the fears were groundless. With her own fire well ablaze, and Whiskers snuggling down beside her, she put the shades and the great silence at naught. It seemed to her that Tearle was close at hand, and where Tearle was there was no room for fear.

'You'll see your master soon, Whiskers,' she murmured, patting him gently as they sat beside her fire after the meal. 'And he doesn't know it! There's a light in your eye, you rascal. I believe you know all about everything!'

In the embers of the fire came memories – mixed memories that alternately hurt and comforted. Somewhere in advance Tearle, too, might be sitting as she was, wistfully dreaming of things, perhaps wanting her still.

That he made a clean breast of what rankled in his brain she could appreciate. He had wanted her to do that, and because she had not, it had lowered her in his eyes. Love should have no skeleton in the closet. He had made an effort to get her to. He was waiting for it, hoping for it, but in her innocence she had not understood. The hot blood mounted as she thought of the unspeakable motive with which she had credited him. She ought to have known that Tearle was not that kind of man. How could she have depreciated his implicit trust in her? Oh, miserable, miserable!

She slept that night as she had not slept for many nights and awoke to find it snowing hard. But that was no deterrent to her now, acclimatized and experienced as she had come to be, provided she could remember the trail. After breakfast she started off with a wild whoop and, to her glee, succeeded in cracking the whip like an old-timer.

The heart within her was as gay as the bells on Whiskers' collar. The snow blew into her eyes and mouth and lay inches thick on dogs and sled, but still she drove on giving voice to the old cry of the snows: 'Mush – mush!'

Late in the afternoon, she saw through the snowy curtain a conical shape ahead; a tent. She urged on the team and in a short time stopped in front of it in the midst of the swirling white kicked up by her animals. Her heart leaped. She had come straight to him. How well she remembered the tent with that small triangular mended patch near the opening! It was Tearle's. A fire burning near the door was almost out, and beside it were cooking utensils. She tumbled from the sled and ran forward.

'Douglas!' she called eagerly.

No reply. She peeped inside the tent and her heart went cold at the sight of a figure lying on a blanket. A second later she was on her knees staring into the unconscious, ashen face of her husband.

'Dead!' she moaned. 'No – no! It can't be! I won't let it be! Douglas! Why don't you speak? Why–?'

A sigh quivered from the stiffened lips. Then thick incoherent speech. She saw his brow was wet with perspiration and when she gently touched it found it burning hot.

'Fever!' she gasped, as the full significance flooded over her. What to do in such a case she did not know. That Douglas could possibly be ill seemed unbelievable, yet there he was muttering strange things and moving his head from side to side. Near him was a second blanket which he had presumably thrown off. She drew it over him, adding yet another from her own supply.

She did not want to leave him alone for a moment, but the snarls of the dogs outside roused her to other duties. Then commenced her time of Calvary. Hurriedly she fed them and made up the fire, running in every few seconds to take a glance at the sick man. Towards night he was worse. That was obvious enough despite her ignorance of illness. He would suddenly sit up and stare into nothingness, then rave wildly about everything from balloons to bear-skins, until her heart cried out for him.

There was no rest that night for her. She sat close beside him watching while he was still, and pleading gently with him when he became delirious. His apparent weakness brought tears to her eyes. He who had been so strong now like a babe in her arms.

Thrice over she paid for any folly of her own when she heard him muttering about her; always about her! 'What a fool – fool– To give her up when– What's that? You lied, Mainwaring – she couldn't do it – why, Susan, we – might have been so happy. It's me – me to blame. Don't leave me again – don't–'

He was hushed to silence in her arms and laid gently back to sigh himself into temp-orary silence. But he would be at it again after the respite, reviving little bits of the past, gesticulating weakly and heaping coals of fire upon her head. But in the midst of his wild talk she could see gleaming brightly the fire of love which had been lighted long ago.

Shortly before the dawn, she succeeded in forcing some warm weak tea between his lips. Whether this was right or wrong she did not know, but it had the effect she desired. Thereafter he slept for four hours. Tired as she was, there was no time for rest. She went to the wood and cut some branches for the fire and then fed the hungry dogs, and half-heartedly started to prepare a meal for herself. She felt no hunger, but common sense told her she must conserve her strength and energy in this crisis, and that food, however little appetite she might have, was necessary. She was forcing herself to eat when a low moan came from the tent.

She ran inside to find him lying perfectly still with his eyes closed. But he seemed to have ceased breathing! She thrust her hand down under the blankets. There was no sign of a heart-beat. Her own startled cry brought reason, and subconsciously she remembered the small mirror she carried. With hands that trembled she held it before his lips and a low cry of joy issued from her lips strained with mental agony when she saw it blurred with his breath. He lived!

Though she had no way of guessing it, her husband had reached the crisis. He was on the borderline between life and death, and the slightest pull might take him either way. She put her face close to his to murmur in his ear, hoping that the whisper might penetrate to the weary brain and be understood in some subconscious fashion.

'Douglas, dear, don't leave me all alone. I've come to make you happy. If you leave me I want to die too. Can't you remember that night when you held me – like this, and we talked of beautiful things? We can make them come true, if you only try. You – mustn't give up – you mustn't.' Her voice rose as she went on with eager passion. 'You can't! I won't let you go – I *won't!*'

Hours may have passed before her exhausted lips ceased to croon to him. All reckoning of time had long since gone. But of a sudden it seemed she was aware that his breast was heaving regularly and the heat of his brow seemed less. Was it possible the worst was over? That conviction was forced upon her at last. She dropped on her knees with her hands clasped, and there came from her soul as well as her eyes a torrent of glad tears.

'Susan!'

The low exclamation came from the man on the bed. She lifted her tear-stained face to see Tearle's eyes moving under his knitted brow.

'I – thought – I thought–!'

Eagerly she reached out to grasp his hand as though she would never let go.

'Don't talk – don't do anything but get well,' she begged.

'Get well!' he muttered, surprised in his weak tones.

'You've been ill,' she whispered. 'Try to go to sleep – please, please.'

'Here, I'm going to get up.'

To his wife's horror he flung the blankets off and tried to raise himself. She rushed at him and caught his tottering form in her arms as he collapsed.

'Don't you understand?' she cried tearfully.

He lay gazing at the soft arms that were around his shoulder. Though he was coming to understand about his illness this other unaccustomed thing was beyond his reason. He put his hand on hers and let it move to and fro caressingly.

'Susan, you *did* go away, didn't you?'

She nodded.

'And now you've come back?'

'Yes, yes – but don't talk. Lie down and let me put the blanket over you.'

He did as she ordered him, still gazing at her wonderingly as she tucked the blankets about him.

'Now you'll sleep!' she admonished, much in the tone she might have employed to an ailing child.

'Why?'

'Because I say so.'

'Very well.' He sighed, content for that time.

That he might more quickly obey her, she went outside and finished her interrupted meal, after reheating it. When she stole to the tent to have a look at her patient she found him sleeping peacefully. Her own brain was aching for sleep, so she stretched a blanket on the ground and was asleep almost as soon as she lay down.

It was nearly dark when she awoke, and the fire was getting low. She flung some wood into it and crept into the tent to see if Tearle were awake.

'Hello, Susan!'

He was sitting up in bed and she rejoiced to notice that the ashen look had left his face.

'How are you feeling?' she asked.

'Better. I guess I've shaken off the fever. Have you been away from camp? I kept calling–' a bit shamefacedly.

'I was asleep,' she replied. 'I felt so tired.'

He nodded understandingly.

'I guess you didn't get much sleep last night.'

'Not much.'

'None. I thought someone was here, but I didn't know who it was. You were talking – talking.'

'Was I?' she murmured, her eyes averted, as she wondered what moment he might make out what she had said.

'Yep. I couldn't tell what it was all about though. It was like as if you were talking from a mountain peak. Gee, I don't want to get that way again.'

She nodded understandingly.

'I'll be all right to-morrow.'

'You won't. You've got to take things quietly for a few days yet. Can you manage to eat anything, do you think?'

'Sure! You try me.'

But while he disposed of a basin of soup and some canned fruit, he was puzzled over the unexpectedness of things. Susan knew it, too, but anxious as she was to tell him the cause, she determined to say nothing until he was well again.

'I guess you missed the boat, or something!' he remarked.

'Something like that,' she demurred.

'But did you come back on foot?'

'No. I bought that dog-team back from the dealer. I guessed you were on your way to Shaggin's and followed that trail.'

'But why?' he muttered. 'That's what gets me guessing.'

'I'll tell you why some other time.'

'Why not now?'

'It's no time to talk about that, Douglas. You're ill and weak still. Don't ask me anything now. I'm at least going to stay here until you are well – if you will let me.'

He nodded reflectively and considered it just as well to put no more questions then. It was later in the evening that he saw her come in and take his sleeping-bag from the corner.

'What's this?' he asked.

'I didn't know you were awake. I – I thought I would not trouble to erect the other tent. It is not so cold to-night.'

'Too cold for you to sleep in the open.'

'Do you think so? Then I had better put up the other tent.'

'Why?'

'Well, I must sleep somewhere!'

His mouth moved nervously as he met her eyes squarely.

'Are you afraid of me, Susan?' he asked soberly.

'I thought it was you who were afraid of me.'

'Not now,' he said, and underneath was a laugh of happiness. 'Please don't go.'

She, too, laughed, and flung the sleeping-bag away. That night she slept within a few feet of him. The first time!

CHAPTER TWENTY-FIVE

For two whole days it snowed. Snowed and snowed until it lay two feet deep over everything. Then the clouds lifted and the bounteous sunshine came to flood the virgin landscape. Tearle's progress towards health was miraculous. On the third evening he was sitting before the fire looking much as he had before the fever laid him low.

Susan watched him with an interest that held much of the maternal.

'You're all right now?' she asked anxiously.

'Fine. Thanks to my wife. You're a tiptop nurse, Susan.'

'It wasn't anything I did,' she demurred. 'You can thank your own wonderful stamina.'

In the brooding silence that followed, the eternal question was knocking at his brain. At last he gave voice to it.

'Why did you come back, Susan?' he asked bluntly.

'You didn't expect me to?'

'No.'

'And didn't want me to?'

He fumbled with his pipe and gazed into the fire.

'I guess I'm a pretty darn fool,' he temporised.

'I'm not so sure,' said Susan slowly, ignoring the lack of compliment.

'What do you mean by that?'

Minutes went by before his wife answered or spoke. Her whole gaze was focused on the reddened embers as though from them to gain inspiration for what she wanted to say, and say it rightly. When she began, her words came haltingly; uncertainly.

'I think,' her slow voice said, 'that I can answer you best by telling you a story. Will you listen all through? Let me finish?'

He nodded acquiescence, but his eyes held curiosity.

'Well, then,' she took a deep breath and started again, her eyes never wavering from the fire, never turning towards him, though she felt the start that quivered through his whole being at the explosion of her first words, 'there were once three girls, who at an early age were left alone in the world. All they possessed were a few hundred pound and a little talent in diverse directions. They were great friends, and having lost their parents in a terrible catastrophe, the bond between them was very strong. Two of them were sisters, and the other–'

'You,' he whispered sympathetically. 'But why–?'

Susan, not appearing to have noticed the

interruption, went on.

'When three girls live alone and depend upon themselves for their livelihood, there comes a certain amount of intolerance towards conventions – love and what not. Their lot was pretty hard, and I think they grew a little hard too. They were up against a pretty big thing – the fight for existence, and it took a lot of sentiment out of them. Almost the only sentiment they had was their love for one another. That was genuine enough, and to them it was sufficient. Well, things got worse financially. They were plagued with bills and demands for rent. They worked themselves weary and still could not meet them. Then one fell sick and the other two had to support her. That brought them near the end of their tether. Something had to be done to stave off disaster. The eldest girl, Edith, hit upon an idea.'

Tearle flinched as he saw what was coming. Once he put up a hand to stop her, but she went on in a level voice, unheeding if she did see.

'The proposal was that one should marry a fairly well-to-do man and care for the other two until they were able to support themselves. It was a miserable, heartless suggestion, but they were desperate. So they decided to exploit. They gambled to decide the – the victim.'

'And it was you,' growled Tearle. 'I know

all about–'

Susan Tearle looked up from the fire to meet her husband's gaze, clear-eyed, as though for the first time she was acknowledging the tale she told held any personal significance.

'You don't know all,' she disagreed, with a shake of her head. 'What you don't know is that when that one – well, I, if we must put it that way – discovered a man who appeared to possess all that was necessary, the whole scheme went wrong. The whole trouble was that I – well – I – fell in love with him! For the first time in my life I knew what love really meant.'

'Susan!' The cry came from the man's long-hurt soul.

'After that, such a vile scheme was impossible of fulfilment. I told the girls I would have nothing more to do with it. I wanted to be married for love only; without any other consideration. When at last I was married I forgot every word about that hideous compact. It was only a few days ago that someone out of the past reminded me of it.'

'Someone out of the past!'

'Mainwaring. He is in Vancouver. He – he told me something I did not know; the thing that perhaps has ruined my happiness and yours.'

'He told you that I knew of that – that business.'

'Yes,' she choked. 'And all this time you have remembered it and believed that I was that type of woman.'

Tearle's face told the story of his tremendous agitation. The knotted muscles bulged as he strove to put his side of the case.

'It wasn't all you,' he said magnanimously. 'I acted like a fool and a beast. When Mainwaring brought me that diary I think I went mad. By then I had a suspicion that you did not guess I was down and out. I was going to tell you that – to ask you to wait until I made good, when – when that thing happened. I was skunk enough to believe that all your words and actions were so much acting. I wanted to hurt you as you had hurt me. Have I hurt you – much?'

'Yes,' she had to admit, a low-voiced apologetic admission, but she added quickly, 'but only because I didn't understand.'

'I know, Susan, but you can have the comfort of knowing I hurt myself more – when I let you go. When you went to the station I–' He hesitated, then he blurted out:

'Well, I could have bitten my tongue off, that's all! Out of plain cussedness I had given up all that mattered in life. I knew I was going to be lonely, but I never guessed how lonely a fellow can be. When I fell sick, I just hoped I never would open my eyes again!'

312

'Douglas!' cried his wife, shocked. 'I can't bear you to speak like that.'

In his own silent, brooding way he said nothing for the next few moments when he was planning his question.

'Susan,' he asked wistfully, 'if that hadn't happened and I had told you just how things were with me would you have waited?'

'For twenty years, if need be. But I didn't want to wait.'

'Gosh! And I never knew! What a mule! That was what was in my mind when I first told you how I cared. I didn't think I had a right to ask a girl like you to give up what you were used to before – before Mainwaring – I reckon my planning to marry you offhand to make you pay for what I thought was my humiliation was just part of my madness. What a mess a man can make of his life by his damned pride!'

He stopped, then his eyes shifting in her direction as though he feared his answer, he added more slowly:

'I guess the time for waiting is past now, eh, Susan? But if you felt you could give me hope, just the smallest chance, I'd sure get going some. I've got nothing – nothing to offer you now, but maybe if you'd give me a year, I'd do something worth while. Could you wait a year?'

She shook her head.

'Why should I wait?' she asked with finality.

'You're right.' Tearle uttered a deep sigh of disappointment. 'Why should you wait when I have wasted so much of your life?'

'Wasted! Douglas, do you imagine all these months have been wasted! I've tasted life – just the outer crust of it, it's true, but still it was life! I never really lived back there in that village. I know what it means now to toil with some object in view.'

'Didn't you have an object away back?'

'Yes, myself; my little ambitions. But living for one's self is not enough. You ask me to wait a year. I tell you I can't wait a week.'

'I – I don't get you,' he muttered.

'If – *if* I said I would wait all that time, what difference would it make?'

'I'd find a home for you. I'd get a farm – somehow – and have it all ready for you. I'd take Shaggin at his word and go felling timber like a machine until I had the dollars. Oh, I'd get 'em if I knew you were waiting.'

'I believe you would. But we're married *now*.'

'We could forget that until–'

'I don't want to forget it.'

He stared at her in perplexity, then a smile, such a smile as seldom had gladdened his eyes in recent months, lit his countenance as he came towards his wife.

'But that wasn't a real wedding we had, was it?'

'It was,' said the woman, and the decisive nod of her head emphasized her words. 'Dreadfully real. Douglas, suppose that farm were ready now – waiting for us – what then?'

'It's not wise to dream.'

'It's no dream,' she replied seriously. 'It is waiting now – a dozen farms, from which you can choose any one you wish. Oh, don't look at me as though you thought my poor brain unsettled. What I'm telling you is true. You invited me to wait a year to come to your farm. I now invite you to wait for less than that to come to mine. Do you refuse?'

Her radiant eyes looked up at him and her two hands rested on his shoulders. He gave a great gulp and his arms went round her to press her closely to him.

'Susan,' he cried, eagerly as a boy, 'do you mean you don't want your freedom? Do you really mean it?'

'I won't have anything that takes me away from my husband.'

Her tremulous red lips were but a few inches below his. With a sigh that was tribute to dreams come true, he dropped his head and kissed her again and again until the whole world was blotted out.

'You love me – you love me! Tell me that!' he begged at last.

'I do love you, dear,' she murmured obediently. 'I've always loved you. Even

315

when misunderstanding made you cold towards me. I'll love you when I'm old and grey and our children are older than we are now.'

'Our children!'

'I love you so, dear. I'll keep nothing – nothing from you; not even my thoughts. There must never be a misunderstanding again.'

'Never – never! But about the farm. That is a misunderstanding, I guess. We've nothing, Susan – yet.'

'Oh, I nearly forgot. Yes, we have. I haven't told you about it, that's all. I am no longer a penniless wife. I am shortly to come into the fortune of a dead relative. You see before you an heiress,' and she dimpled delightedly as she dropped him a mock curtsy.

His eyes opened wide at this astonishing news, but the next instant his mouth tightened. She wagged her finger warningly.

'I know exactly what is on your tongue,' she chided. 'But let me tell you now, my fortune goes with me or I do not go at all.'

'But–!'

'Douglas,' she murmured. 'All the wasted time, as you called it, was brought about through a wretched misunderstanding concerning money. Are we going to let it happen again? To me, this fortune means nothing. If we had to tramp Canada from end to end I'd still be happy with you. Don't let this be a curse. What we hold we hold jointly all the while we have each other.'

'Maybe you're right,' he conceded, reluctantly. 'But it all seems like a dream that can't last.'

'It can – it shall.'

They sat down by the fire his arm round her, her head on his shoulder. From out of the darkness a pair of green eyes shone weirdly.

'Whiskers!' she called.

'Don't call him!'

'Why not?'

'Oh, I'm sure jealous to-night. I don't want anyone or anything else near.'

'You dear silly thing!'

'It may be different after to-night, but this is our night. I guess we were really married just now for the first time.'

'And this is our honeymoon.'

In the fullness of their hearts, words were a superfluity. They sat there, heart communing with heart in the vast stillness of the great woods. They had taken no account of time when Douglas Tearle roused himself and his newly found wife with a short mirthful laugh. She glanced up at him inquiringly.

'What is it, dear?' she asked.

'I just happened to think,' chuckled Tearle, 'about a friend of mine in Vancouver. Reckon may be he's thinking about how I had a pipe dream about having a wife.'

'Why–' began Susan, wondering.

'Why, just that I wired this here Jim Todd to keep an eye on you, and let me know when your money was gone. I wasn't taking no chances with that uncle.'

Susan Tearle reached up to pat her husband's cheek. Her cup of happiness was full. It had only needed this; the knowledge that he had never intended to allow her to go out into the world penniless in spite of her pride.

'Look! Whiskers has gone back to sleep. He knows I am safe with you.'

'You always were.'

'Yes, I think I was.'

Night came down, and the stars watched them as they sat there talking of the magic future, building castles high up into the blue. Then during one of their periods of silence, Tearle looked down to find her asleep in his arms. He lowered his head to kiss her tenderly on the brow. She opened her eyes and smiled up at him.

'Time we went to bed,' he murmured.

'I – I suppose it is,' she yawned, smiling sleepily.

Douglas Tearle rose and lifted his wife tenderly in his arms, and carried her into their tent.